Winter Tales

A Cold-Weather Anthology

**A Collaboration
Between
Horwich Writers' Cauldron
Adlington Writing Group and
Write You Are**

First published by
Scott Martin Productions, 2019
www.scottmartinproductions.com

First published in Great Britain in 2019 by
Scott Martin Productions
10 Chester Place,
Adlington, Chorley, PR6 9RP
scottmartinproductions@gmail.com
www.scottmartinproductions.com

Electronic version and paperback versions available for purchase
on Amazon.

Introduction, Previously Published and Dedications

The publisher would like to thank Penny Taylor for her stunning lino prints on the cover and throughout. We would also like to thank all those who contributed to this volume. Your writing and companionship are greatly valued.

Please note that a few of these pieces of writing have been previously published, and this will be mentioned at the end of those works.

Lesley Atherton of Scott Martin Productions, would like to dedicate this book to writers and creative people everywhere. May we long enjoy the colder season and make the most of the creative times it grants us.

Contents

A Bloomer
by Pat Laurie

Heidi had not quarrelled in fifty odd years
with her partner and friend, Gertie Day,
but she came to her limit, a right bitter end,
when Gertie gave her knickers away.

Yes, Heidi had compassion for perishing bums,
but those drawers were her best fleecy-lined;
the acme of fashion, had cost quite a sum,
how could Gertie believe she'd not mind?

All right, so the fashion was in 1914 but
knickers made then sure would last,
with reinforced gusset and the sweetest
frills in russet and
modest and voluminous with guide-ropes holding fast.

Sad Heidi berated her faithless friend, Gert:
'You've given my bloomers away! What will
be next, my stays and my vest? My precious
lisle stockings or my wool negligee?'

'Oh Heidi, I'm sorry. Forgive me. Please do,'
begged Gertrude, all broken and spent.
See, these clowns they came round, from
the circus I'll be bound.
And gave me loads of money for your keks...
to make a tent'.

A Christmas Adventure
by Christine Wilkinson

Edwina Bear was feeling very sad. Nobody had picked her off the shelf for Santa's toy collection for two whole years, apart from Dilly Elf, who only do so to dust her once a week. Her gently flick with the duster and soothing words made Edwina feel needed.

All of a sudden Edwina noticed that Doug, the Boss Elf, was pointing at her.

'What can this mean?' she thought. 'Am I past my sell by date, and will be put in a large green box with the other toys who have been here a long time?'

'What will happen to me now?' thought Edwina. 'Will I be taken to the rubbish tip? Or to a charity shop, where the old ladies will respect me? Or, it could be wonderful if I could go to a home where the children have no toys to play with, and I could share a big hug with them.'

Stealthily, Doug Elf approached the shelf with Dilly.

'Wow! Two of them. Whatever is going on?' thought Edwina.

Carefully, Dilly Elf picked her up and gave her a few nice feathery flicks with her duster. Doug Elf then placed her in a bright yellow box.

'Time to go to your new home, Edwina Bear. Santa, Dilly and I have been waiting for a special place for you for two years, and at last your time has come. I won't bore you with the details, but we all hope you have some fun.'

Edwina was then covered with a soft, blue fleece.

'Good luck,' Dilly said, looking very sad. 'I wish I could come with you.'

'I shall miss you too.'

Once the box was closed, Edwina took out a magic tool. She'd stolen it from Billy's bench, while she was having her last dust down by Dilly Elf.

With great precision, Edwina made a little peep hole in the bottom right hand corner of the box.

Sneaking a peek through the hole, she noticed that at least five different sized boxes were being loaded on to an old supermarket trolley, and that they were being loaded by a strange old woman with a pointed nose. She was dressed in a lilac cloak and sported a feather in her pointed hat.

Suddenly, Edwina felt a bump, as the trolley was loaded onto the omnibus, where there was a bearded old man. His feet didn't touch the ground as he perched on his very high seat. The wizened, bearded old man wore a small, pointed cap on his head. With his long, strong arms, he pushed down a long handle, and the omnibus shot into the air with a whoosh.

The bus then flew past Santa on his sleigh. He was on his way to deliver the presents to a large oak tree, where anxious parents and friends waited to collect the toys for their family. They waited there as they didn't have any chimneys for Santa to climb down.

'Times are changing,' thought Edwina Bear.

Suddenly there was a plop as the lilac bus landed and righted itself up in the grounds of a very old-looking building, where outside the trees were covered in glistening snow.

Lilac Letitia took a very large key out of her pocket and unlocked a crumbly ancient door. As it opened, Edwina noticed a large glass cabinet filled with toys.

'Welcome to your new homes, Edwina Bear, Susie Doll, Peter Puppet, Jonny Dog, Gemima Mouse, and my favourite, Buckles the Cheshire Cat. I own a small toy museum which is open to the public on Sundays, school holidays and bank holidays – especially Christmas Eve. I also sell healing and other special herbs to those people who bring their children. The money keeps me in lilac feathers, which I buy for my hat from the ostrich farm.'

On the night before Christmas Eve, when all the families had gone home, Letitia was making her midnight security rounds when she noticed that the single cabinet door, where Edwina was usually placed, was slightly ajar.

Peering inside she noticed that Edwina Bear was not there!!!

I wonder: Who has stolen Edwina Bear? Do you know, children?

Autumn
by Sally James

Autumn crackles in gutters
blows across cobbles
falls like amber confetti
on to woodland paths.
I wade ankle deep in rustle
wrap myself in mist
let embers of ancient fires
warm me, before frost
ignites the moon
invites winter.

A Winter's Blessing
by Jayne Schofield

Winter time I welcome you
Into my life, do what you will,
I honour all you bring to me.
I wish you peace. So mote it be.

Autumn Departure
by Neville Southern

The light of life is strange late in the year:
Moons go quickly, eves and night times stay.
Mist and twilights linger on
Throughout the livelong day.

It's in autumn that the gales begin
To strip summer's flesh to stark bones.
Though with scarlet hips and haws
And coppery chestnut tones.

The leaves on the ground are amber and brown
And bulrushes blacken the reeds;
Moorland heathers are purple and blue mists
Soften the bright colours and brilliant beads.

The nests of birds can now be seen;
They and the squirrels gather in delight
On fruit and seed to feed and hoard
Though harvest's past its height.

Crashing waves on harsh cold shores
The calling of birds southward flying
Signal in lamentation loud
That this old year is dying.

Nature seeks an ongoing truce with time
To seal the wounds from wintertime and frost,
Only in spring to start again
A was by no means lost.

We can only believe through leaves are falling
And flowers and plants are withering,
They only wait through wintery hours
The coming of the spring.

When my time comes, I will follow the birds,
Disappearing into the clouds and rain,
Leaving my former life behind
To be in flight again.

A Snowy Day
by Kath Litherland

Drifting into being,
Weightless, aimless, towards the final goal.
Perfect! Whole – a part of a whole.
Radiant; reflecting myriad lights, fragmented
Colours, all colours, scintillant shards of
Prisms and rainbow structures,
Cells bond in unique patterns of
Fragile strength;
Cluster and coalesce for a moment in time;
Freedom to move, to feel the pull
Of conflicting forces, a temporary straying
From a path that is one's whole intention;
Following and flowing,
Leading and showing;
Gathering together in a harmony of purpose,
Sharing a unity of design; uniquely individual,
A prospect of destination,
Meandering through meaning,
Untroubled, accepting, delighting in mission.
Moments and eons,
Fractals and fractions,
One and all one;
Existence and ending.

A Winter's Day in the Hills
by David Jackson

We park the car by the farm, and start to walk up the snow covered track, past the cottages where a girl who would become a writer once watched her grandmother bake 'Singing Hinnies'. The snow is thick, and the way up the hill is a ribbon of ice, more frozen stream than path.

Time is thickly layered here; below us an old chapel with strange Masonic inscriptions, to our right an Iron Age fort, higher up the slope a Bronze Age burial site and finally, our goal, the abandoned farmstead of Blaewearie.

We pass through the gate and climb upwards, alongside the steep, tree-topped ramparts of the Iron Age fort. We leave the valley and walk out onto the flattened tops of the moorland. The snow is deep here, and the path hard to follow. Ahead of us we can see the ruins of the steading, the roofless house and barn standing in its grove of trees at the foot of the rock outcrop.

Two miles later, we are close to the Bronze Age burial cists, and she says we should make a detour to look at the ring of stones standing in the snow. But it's too cold to tarry, and we hurry back to the main path. I try a short cut, but misjudge my way and sink to my waist in a deep drift. Her laughter rings out over the moor.

'You always fall into something' she says, remembering my tumble that midnight when we'd come up here to watch the stars and took the wrong way down. Somehow, I find myself back on my feet on firm snow and heading on towards the steading.

We pass the point on the track where in late spring the young adder slithered across our path, too quick even to catch on camera. We pass the stream that runs down into the valley, we can't see it, but we hear it gurgling under the snow.

Now, we have reached the steading and enter the flat platform of land that used to be the farmyard. To our left are the ruined buildings and we walk on over the bank where in younger days one late summer's evening we sat and made plans for a very different future. We pass the ancient plum tree whose fruit we gather each autumn. Before us lies the wall of rocks that encircle the secret garden, hewn out for a Victorian farmwife all those years before, the initials of long departed farmers carved into the stones. Ahead is the flight of steps that will take us up the wall and down into the garden, and on to the alder shrouded pool beyond.

The great beech tree that, all the years we have come here, has stood guardian over the entrance lies fallen in front of us. It lies half covered in snow, like the body of a slaughtered giant at Ragnarok.

The tree had seemed a permanent feature of the landscape but on this year's first visit, following the spring gales, we found that it blown down, lying on its side, its massive roots upended, and its branches smashed and shattered. The winds that give this place its name finally triumphed over it, and brought it down.

It was a shock, she'd cried, it had seemed so permanent and we felt that something important had been lost, like losing a friend.

But now she stands, at the top of the steps, in her green coat, her face pink with the cold and the joy she always feels in this place. 'Take my photo,' she calls.

We don't tarry long in the abandoned garden, and move out, through the snow covered bracken, seeking the pool beyond. A perfect circle, ringed with alder saplings, it is an eerie, magical place, a place for myths and moonlight meetings. Today the pool is frozen, and she sits for a while entranced by the patterns of ice crystals forming on the reeds.

But we cannot stay. Winter days are short, and the darkness is falling. Reluctantly, we leave the pool and retrace our steps down the hill, back to the waiting car, and the journey back to our hotel in the coastal village, where the preparations for the evening's festivities will have already begun. Tonight, as the church clock strikes midnight, we'll stand on the beach, by the lighthouse, and watch the fireworks.

A New Year beckons. Which way will the world turn this time?

(An earlier version of this piece was runner up in Writers' Forum's flash fiction competition in July/Aug 2018)

A Wintery Tale
by Christine Wilkinson

Living alone in a cold, dark room.
There was an old lady swishing a broom.
Huddled in a tattered cloak of black,
Collecting her dust in a hessian sack.
Ready for her next customer to come,
To pick up their herbal tea and rum.

Another side-line she had to sell,
Herbal brewed potions to make people well.
Enabling them to survive the winter blast.
In frosty conditions they arrived at last.
They came in twos and threes and more
Bringing fresh eggs. Rabbits to barter for.
Some previous products for Meg to last the winter long,
Where she hibernates in her little crooked cottage,
Where she belongs.

Down in the valley, very close to the busy cotton mill,
A stone's throw from the ascent of Pendle Hill.

Advertising Feature
by David Jackson

Do your family really want your company over Christmas? Can you stand three continuous days with your nearest and dearest (I'm referring to the cost of their presents obviously)?

If the answer's 'No' then why not swop the warmth and comfort of your suburban home for our desolate windswept, rain sodden hillside and spend the season with us here at the Hotel Kirkegaard.

After spending Christmas Eve making your way through the hordes of drunks, displaced grannies and depressed daughters-in-law making their sullen ways up the 200 mile car park that is the M6, you'll be welcomed by our minimum waged East European staff who are overjoyed to have been asked to sacrifice their own Yuletide in order to pander to your every need.

Sit yourself down with a mince pie and a glass of brandy before a blazing log fire and watch, through the picture windows, the ever changing display made by the head- and tail-lights on the motorway below.

As we're at least 40 miles from the nearest shop so you have every excuse to stop worrying about that present you forgot to buy for the woman four doors down. Also, as the nearest church is 20 miles away there's no opportunity for religion to interfere with the main purpose of Christmas – that being to stuff as much food and drink into your face as you can.

And that's where we come in.

Settle into your sumptuously appointed bedroom (with en-suite), scoff the complimentary chocolates and quaff down the welcoming bottle of (warm, Aldi) Prosecco we leave there for you. Then come down to the lounge where more mince pies, stollen cake and savoury nibbles (every Lidl counts) will keep you munching until it's time for a Christmas Eve feast prepared by our award-winning chef. It was actually a bronze Duke of Edinburgh's award, but still, an award is an award.

After dinner our resident comedian Genghis leads the staff in a variety show. You'll laugh uproariously at his antics and jokes. (You will know when to laugh as his attractive female assistant holds up a notice saying 'laugh NOW!) As an example of Genghis' humour - 'Plato and a Platypus go into a bar. The barman says 'What's with her?' and Plato says 'I know, but she looked all right in the cave'.

Genghis used to be a Philosophy lecturer back home in Minsk.

The bar is open until 2.00 am or you can have a bottle or two taken up to your room to keep you going.

Next morning (Christmas Day) begins with a sumptuous all-you can-eat breakfast buffet, after which you may feel ready for an invigorating walk through the adjacent fields. We would however advise against this as the local gentry are a bit trigger happy and a blast of buckshot in the nether regions does tend to dampen the Christmas spirit.

Christmas lunch is a 12 course affair, with a different wine accompanying each course, and with liqueurs and coffee at the end.

At this juncture you may be getting a little anxious as to the effects of all this eating and drinking, but don't be perturbed in any way. The hotel has its own in-house defibrillator and our staff are all trained in coronary resuscitation techniques. If the worst comes to the worst, we have our own fully equipped ambulance to whisk you off to the highly rated local Cardiac Care Unit (though local may be stretching it a bit as it's 60 miles away and may be closed at Christmas.)

After lunch, why not repair to the TV lounge where, just to give the right atmosphere of Christmases past we have *The Great Escape* and *The Charge of the Light Brigade* on a continuous loop. And of course, the bar's open all day!

Naturally, as we are a modern hotel, we also have a fully equipped gym, swimming pool and sauna in the annexe. Maybe you'd like to try that. No-one has yet, but our manager lives in hope.

For those who survive the afternoon, we lay on an evening buffet at which you can fill any spaces you may have left in your digestive system. We also provide a wide range of indigestion remedies, painkillers and liver salts in every bedroom.

And of course, from 8.00 pm Genghis returns (as

unfortunately do many of his jokes).

Boxing Day is pretty much a repeat of Christmas Day, but we do exchange *The Charge of the Light Brigade* for *It's a Wonderful Life* – which is an improvement, we feel.

On Day Three, breakfast is served bright and early. There's an eclectic menu as the kitchen staff are desperately trying to use up all the odd items left over in the larders.

Please try to be prompt at breakfast and with your packing and departure, as we close the hotel at 12.30 pm so that our (newly unemployed and now homeless) staff can catch their trains at Penrith on their way to a well-earned (if unpaid) holiday.

If you experience any feelings of dread or anxiety at the thought of such a hedonistic adventure, have no nerves – for, as our founder has said – anxiety is (just) the dizziness of freedom.

So, don't delay, book today!

An Emotional Earthquake
by Jackie Hutchinson

Mother's Wrath!

So appalled by your vicious tongue,
remarks so hurtful, they stung;

such festering hate –
well, now it's too late;

we can never go back
after your verbal attack!

It's time to step away,
feeling shock and dismay.

As I've matured into adulthood,
achieving things you didn't think
 I could.
I stand back and recognise
how intelligent and wise,
I've become without your care
or intimidating stare!

Before the Fall
by Dave Jackson

The site lies silent
The snow that fell in the night
Covers the ground in a cotton-wool blanket
Hiding the squalor and debris the winter has brought
Leaving all clean and white
Re-making the world anew

Yet on Mick's plot, around the chicken run
There are footprints
A vixen and her cubs, looking for a winter meal
We follow their tracks
They circle every hen coop
Death stalks the site

Perhaps, when we return tomorrow
The snow will be stained with blood and feathers
The remnants of a kill, the evidence of slaughter
But today, in this early morning light
All is clean and white
The world has been made anew.

Blacky Tops
by Roy Bennett

Oh, all you little Blacky tops,
Pray, don't you eat my father's crops
Whilst I lie down to take a nap.
For if he should come with his cocked hat
And his long gun
Then you must fly and I must run.

Boxed Up on Bodmin For Xmas
by Roy Bennett

It was nearly Xmas. I had just finished a job as the warden of a youth hostel in Cornwall. Being a wandering kind of a soul, I had decided to have a meander around the west country. The weather was crisp but sunny. It seemed good for a couple of days of biking and camping, before making on home on public transport, to Lancashire for the festivities.

The forecast said cold spells but hell, you were always warm pedalling a bike, so I set off. I reached the bottom of Bodmin. The sun was shining, and I decided to make it across the moor then either camp or find a hostelry for the night. As I climbed, the weather darkened, and it grew colder. It started to drizzle. I donned my cape and carried on, forever it seemed like. The rain turned to a fine powdery snow. Bike riding had become a precarious mode of transport. As the snow deepened the bike was slipping and sliding all over the place so I had to get off and walk. The wind got up; the snow thickened. Between the drifting snow I spotted a light ahead. Thinking I was going to find a farmhouse or cottage to shelter for the night I quickened my pace, but it turned out to be nothing more than a telephone box. By then it was blizzard conditions. Best make the most of what I've got.

I put the bike against the windy side of the kiosk and covered it with the cape. I managed to make it pretty draught proof, piling snow up against the bottom on all exposed sides. Being prepared for camping I had supplies, a primus stove and sleeping bag. I made myself a cuppa and soon felt snug as a bug in a rug in the steamy atmosphere within. Ready for a kip I hunkered down, lying on my back with my feet up the side of the box. I slept reasonably well all considered. I was able to vary my position, to lying on my side at right angles, when I needed.

Next morning, the snow was halfway up the glass totally blocking me in. I managed to open the door enough to scrape some snow for making a hot drink. Just got it on when – the phone rang! It startled me. A lady asked me if I was such a number.

'No.' I replied. 'I'm in a telephone kiosk on the moors

and I'm snowed in.'

'Don't be silly.' said she, and promptly hung up.

The weather had abated, and I was feeling a bit brighter. I tried to open the door some more but when I did, it was bitterly cold and blowing a hooley, so I drew back into my right royal GPO shelter to keep warm.

The phone rang again. The same lady as before.

'Are you really in a telephone box on the moor?' she asked.

'Yes.' I said.' I'm quite comfortable thank-you.'

She asked me what I had to eat and drink. I explained that I had supplies and a primus and was able to make a hot meal and drink. The tone of the conversation got quite jocular and we hung up on good terms. I got myself ready for my kip in my grand hotel and spent a second night, snug though slightly cramped in the 3' x 3' space.

Next morning, I awoke to the sound of an engine. Outside was a police land-rover and two burly coppers. I bade them good morning. They asked me how I was, and I told them, 'Fine. But I needed some milk.

'Just get your stuff together.' They said. 'It taken us three hours to get here and we are not leaving you.' So, I rode back to the police station sandwiched between the two of them, with my bike, tent and rucksack in the back. We arrived at a tiny village of no more than two dozen cottages, plus the police station.

I was greeted by the woman I had spoken to on the phone. She was a hale, hearty 'Jam and Jerusalem' sort of a lady, in her late forties. She offered me her home as guest over the next few days, including a lovely Xmas. It seems I had become quite the celebrity and I received lots of visitors. The old chaps told tales of the moors and other folks' disastrous endings, reminding me of how lucky I was.

As the weather improved and the roads cleared, I said my farewells and set off again on my bike. My planned two-day journey had become a memorable week and a half.

Cardiac Bypass
by Pat Laurie

My little mother, Frances Victoria,
killed death with kindness, believe it or not.
She wasn't a fool but had mystical blindness
when faced with that challenge, a bold Captain Scott.

She married my father, an invalid, Michael,
so gentle and tender, against all advice.
She thought torrents of loving
would stop haemorraging cycles
of white-born bacilli; her pleas would suffice.

Her practical spirit, in some contradiction,
behoved her to foster harsh hygiene rules:
She scrubbed and she scoured the near-sterile kitchen
and cared for her family, she never downed tools.

She upset the critics by having us children.
'What further folly?' you'd hear them declare:
'Look at young Pattie, notice her pallor?
And Brian, poor babby, it makes you despair'.

Against all the odds we children grew healthy
Despite all expert judgement and sneers.
Yes, life was hard and we never were wealthy
but shielded by warmth there were very few tears.
I cannot emulate my little mother,
her faith and her pride and irrational belief
that loving kills death, disease and all evil
though with her as a guide I should know some relief.

And I can tell lies just as all sinners can
but if true to myself I should be;
I know I'm not nice, I've a sliver of ice in my heart
and my feelings are bipartisan.
I'd pity my enemy, tend to his wounds,
but true, purely, love him? Not me!

Celebration
by Delia Southern

'We can really celebrate Christmas this year, now the war is over,' said Isobel to her father. 'No blackout, no fire-watches, and a few more things in the shops.'

Kay, aged 5, was sitting quietly, looking at a book and listening intently.

'Mmmmm... celebrate,' she thought. 'That means dress up, processions, tea on the green with cake and people being sick. Doesn't sound like Christmas. That was holly and church. Oh yes, and a stocking by the fire – wasn't it?'

Of course, Kay turned out to be right, but what she did not know was that her mum, Isobel had spent every penny available on making this Christmas special for her – her first real Christmas. They had a chicken for Christmas dinner, nuts, oranges and a cake. Kay was entranced by the little tree with old glass baubles and candles on it. She was also overwhelmed by the little pile of presents she received.

Isobel, putting Kay to bed, was happily aware that her day had been successful – a real celebration. But she was flabbergasted when Kay asked 'Mummy. Why is it that I've had presents from Father Christmas and from everyone I know, but nothing from you?' It was not easy to explain, and Isobel never made that mistake again.

Chris's Drinking
by Lesley Atherton

Chris's drinking was getting out of hand. He rubbed his eyes and behind the kaleidoscopes of glowing rubies, emeralds and opals perpetuating on the back of them, behind the flickering blood vessel and the pulsating nerves came an image: an image of two baby reindeer.

Chris's eyes remained closed, squinting in order to see the reindeer more clearly: their grey-white heavy coats, their black outlined ears, and the tiniest hint of antlers. They walked towards him, inquisitive and unafraid, their hooves crunching and compacting the heavy snow beneath, and it was only then that Chris realised that he was outside, and that it had been snowing.

One of the deer said 'Cold'. When Chris didn't respond, he tried again.

'Cold,' he said, and the corners of his mouth turned up in a small smile at Chris's expression. The other reindeer joined him. 'Cold,' the first repeated. The other nodded. 'Yes, isn't it?' he agreed.

Chris tried calling after them, but they seemed not to hear as they moved away, propelled by something more like wind than leg-power. He wanted to know more of where they came from and why they chose to talk to him, but as he reached out they drifted out of his view, carried off on the breeze-borne snow.

Shaking himself awake from what he assumed must have been another of his regular hallucinations, Chris looked up as a tall, thin woman walked past him, scowling down at his filth from inside her fur coat. It had been a long time since Chris had seen such a coat, and he reached to the woman, grunting and desperate to remove it from her and reunite the pelts with their rightful owners. He wanted to shout to her, and to articulate his random thoughts and feelings.

But the woman yelled and ran, and Chris's communication system wasn't working. It rarely was nowadays.

And it seemed like no time later that another, slightly older woman came into his view. Smiling at Chris with her chubby chipmunk cheeks, she took his hand and picked him up, wincing at the stench, but continuing anyway. The woman walked Chris, with his ambling inaccurate strides a couple of streets from where he'd been lying, and through paint-scratched doors into a place he'd never been before. It didn't take long for his eyes to adjust and for him to realise he had been picked up like a bum on the street. Because he was a bum on the street.

He was seated onto a bench and leaned onto a table. 'I'll get you food,' the chipmunk said, as a man with grey eyes and skin jostled him. 'Hey Jack,' the man said, revealing an all-but toothless mouth. His shirt was yellowed and fraying round the neck and was buttoned wrongly.

'Hey,' Chris mumbled, drool leaving his mouth and dripping onto the table. It didn't matter that he wasn't Jack. 'Hey, right, I just saw Rudoph's two little brothers or something.' The longest sentence he'd managed in quite some time.

'Oh yeah, mate,' the grey man said, gurning and scratching his grey overgrown stubble. 'Yeah I see Rudolph all the time, Jack. What's your tipple, mate?'

'Huh?'

'What you drinking?'

'Reindeer piss,' answered Chris with a surly attempt at a grin. The man pushed him so he wobbled on the bench, till Chris was forced to show him the almost empty bottle.

'Wine,' the man commented with a toothless attempt at a whistle. 'Posh bastard.'

Yeah, well, maybe, thought Chris, but the wine was doctored with vodka. So, posher than posh.

Chris tried to get up from the bench then, but his efforts took him stumbling into a foul smelling sofa, then onto the cold hard floor. The other man watched blankly as Chris closed his eyes again, welcoming two little reindeer back to his mind. The larger walked to him, shaking the snow from his hooves and thick coat, leaving talcum powder traces on the tatty tiled floor.

'Evening,' Chris grunted at the reindeer, and took another gulp of the vodka wine concoction. Embrace the madness, he thought. Enjoy the ride, he thought. Reindeer and vodka wine - the best friends you'll ever have, he thought.

'Merry Christmas,' Chris slurred as his head rested on the cold filthy floor and he awaited the sweet, blissful release of intoxicated sleep.

(First published in 'Can't Sleep, Won't Sleep' 4)

Christmas For All
by Christine Wilkinson

In the cold, cold winter's icy blast
Enjoy the freedom while it lasts
Relax before a blazing log fire
Drinking mulled wine, chocolates, your desire
While the howling wind outside does blow
Cobs away from covering snow.

Outside the laughter while children play
Creating snow people on the way
Igloos, houses, and dinosaurs tall
Look out! here comes a flying snowball
Hurtling through the air at rapid pace
Hitting the oldest child on the face.

Others are sledging down the mountain track
Before the snow melts and time to turn back
For home where it's warm and safe inside
Waiting for Santa down the drainpipe to slide
To spread presents around the Christmas tree,
Something for everyone: wait and see.

The Co-operative Milk Collection
by Roy Bennett

Winter 1947. Mom, Dad and I were living on the farm at Jericho, in Bury at that time. I woke up one morning and everything was bright and sparkling. I looked out of my bedroom to a silent wonderland of snow, so deep it was almost reaching the windowsill.

My old man shouted for me to get up, stating the very obvious 'It's snowed!' he said. Downstairs was in darkness. Snow obscured the daylight. We had gas lamps in those days. Mum lit the mantles so we could see. Father meanwhile had gone to the front door and flung it open. There, before him was a wall of white with the impression of the door pressed into it.

'Dorothy… come look at this,' he shouted. With that the snow collapsed on top of him into the kitchen, so setting the mood for the day.

The snow might well have been eleven-foot-deep, but we still had to get cows milked and fed and get the churns to the main road for collection by the Co-operative wagon. To start with, to dig ourselves OUT of the house we had to shovel the snow INTO the kitchen first. Having broken through the crust of snow to let the daylight in so we could see where we could throw the snow out, we then had to get through to the shippon where eight hungry cows were waiting to be milked and fed. All three of us set to, shovelling. It was lucky for us that the shippon doors opened inwards. Father pushed the door open and the heat from the cows wafted out into the snowy passageway. Unfortunately, it caused the sides of the tunnel to collapse inward. Father was covered in snow for a second time.

The dairy was a short way off from the shippon. Dad dug his way through and started the engine, that powered the compressor that powered the milking machine. Meanwhiles, I was busy wiping down the cows' bags.

Next problem… the cows objected to cold hands on their teats. The first bucket of milk was sent flying across the shippon floor by an almighty cow-kick. Poor Pater. Soaked again! More success with the second one. The milk flowed from the milking machine along a pipe to the dairy where it filtered into a huge tun dish. It then ran down a corrugated cooler, not that was needed that particular day. Then it flowed into the milk churns. My job was to watch the milk level in the churns and change them as they got full. The cream on the milk was separated off, into half pint bottles, via a machine with a turning handle. One of my treats was to get a big helping of cream and that day was no different.

It was now about 8:30 am. Normally I would be getting off to school.

'No school for you today, my lad!' Dad announced. I brightened up at that.

The next challenge we faced was to get the churns to the collection stage on the main road, where they would be picked up by the Co-op wagon. From there it would be taken to the main dairy and bottled. The distance from our dairy to the road was the longest quarter of a mile I have ever contended with. We dug from the farm gate to the calf shed, where our very ancient tractor was kept. It was temperamental but Father managed to get it chugging into life. He took it into the farmyard and attached an old square water tank to it. Then he put the churns of milk into the tank and dragged it along the lane. On foot the snow was way over my head but from the tractor I could see over the top of it. These days it might not be so common for a ten-year-old to drive a tractor but back then, no labour source was wasted, and I was expected to. I would drive as far as I could, then get off and help dig away the snow. Finally, we were able to drop the churns off. Father had sat in the water tank dragging behind, to stop the churns falling over and to keep it steady. He was a bit miffed at the speed I drove home and turned around in the yard. I really did not mean to tip him out. He rounded off the morning with yet another dunk in snow. Mum had cooked us a fine breakfast, bacon, eggs and all the trimmings. He felt a lot better after that.

Dark is the Cloister
by Malcolm Timms

The novice monk quietly closes the dormitory door, and steps into the abbey cloister. He is on his way to the kitchen, to light the cooking fires.

A few rush tapers still burn in the gloomy corridor, their inky black, sooty smoke rising torpidly from the yolk coloured flame and casting an eerie yellow light, across the deathly cold, stone floor slabs.

His bare frozen feet momentarily lose their grip and he slips. Not on the spent dirty straw, strewn across the shadowy floor, but on something warm and sticky.

He looks down. A small crimson pool of red glistens, bright in the sickly yellow light.

Is it blood? Should he touch it? Should he bend down and taste it? A wave of nausea flows through his body as he remembers the odd coppery taste of blood, from his childhood, bile rising in his throat, as he takes a step back.

Looking down the corridor he can see more bright splodges of crimson and then droplets, as black as pitch, in the shadow.

A morbid fear grips his body and it takes all his will to force his legs to move on.

As he turns the corner in to the next corridor, ghostly silver shafts of moonlight, pierce the stygian gloom. A gust of icy cold wind stabs through the unglazed windows, like a million ice crystals piercing his mortal flesh.

An owl shrieks in the light of the full moon, announcing its impending flight of death and destruction, in its hunt for prey.

One, then two, then a third of the rush lamps gutter and fail, the black waxy smoke, rising to further blacken the wooden roof timbers. Now, only the shafts of silver, light his way.

Still following as best he can the crimson trail, the young monk rounds the last corner and stops dead in his tracks.

There against the door at the end of the corridor, wreathed in shadow, lurks a stooped hooded figure, clutching a large barrel shaped entity to his portly frame.

The owl rises from its perch, and with a macabre shriek, soars into the night sky. There will be more death and destruction before the night is out.

The young monk takes a tentative step forward.

The apparition throws back his hood and reveals a rictus grin. Jet black obsidian eyes, hooded, beetle browed, transfix the young monk.

A low groan comes first, then a high pitched whine. 'T'Abbot told me not to hide t'light under bushel. Now I've burnt bloody 'ole in it and all me plum jam's leaked out.'

Darkest Night
by Jayne Schofield

Cosy up, sink in,
Curtains closed, remembering
Time's now gone, the past is here
To visit with each passing year.

Fires blaze, lights are bright
As daylight soon gives way to night,
The darkness holds each home below
As spirits call on those they know.

Soups and stews with dumplings too,
Around the table, love filled view,
The sound of laughter, shared delight,
It's warm within this darkest night.

Families!
by Lynne Taylor

Families, as our Fiona would say, what are they like? My friend, Ruth, thinks she's missed out by not having a family. I've told her all she's missed out on is a load of heartache, worry and aggravation, but she doesn't listen. She said that at least I'd been married. She's even missed that.

She's right of course, I have been married. My Jack, ahh, what a man! He was lovely my Jack, until he was so cruelly taken from us. It were fifteen years ago that he was so callously taken, and I still miss him. If I ever get my hands on the thieving bitch that took him, I'll kill her! See what I mean about heartache, worry and aggravation!

I've two sons. Bill's the eldest and Tom's two years younger. They're both good lads.

Our Bill's married to Alice and they've two grown up sons of their own. The eldest, Simon, lives in London but he regularly comes home and their youngest, Peter, lives in Spain. Unfortunately, he doesn't come home as often. But they're both doing well, I think.

Bill retires in a couple of years and what he's going to do with himself when he does the Lord in Heaven knows, but he ain't talking to me. That's Bill isn't talking to me not the Lord in Heaven. I don't think He's ever talked to me! I didn't hear Him anyway if He did, but they keep telling me I need a hearing aid.

No, Bill hasn't talked to me since last Saturday. Him and Alice came round on Sat'day morning to take me out for't day and no sooner had we set off than the heavens opened. Alice didn't fancy traipsing round in't rain and neither did I, so Bill decided to take us to that new art gallery that's opened near the bus station.

Now Bill and art don't go together. You see the problem is he thinks he knows everything about art because he did art appreciation for a year at night school and now he thinks he's an expert! No sooner were we through the door than he started! There's this picture hanging there, you can't miss it, it's in the entrance. It's a bit of white paper with some black splodges on it. Bill said it depicted the fight between good and evil, but I said it looked like it had been painted by monkeys.

Then he started waffling on about another painting. It were all reds and blacks with a few green dribbles. I asked him what that depicted, and he said it were souls descending into the fiery pits of Hell. I told him my soul wasn't green dribble! It's blue! I quite like blue.

The next one looked like a jigsaw puzzle gone wrong, but Bill said it depicted the perfection of the female form. Rubbish, I said, how long has the perfect female had a foot growing out of the top her head, an eye on her belly button and an arm growing out of her nose? He said that the artist had been inspired by Picasso. I said more like inspired by drugs and went off to the café. If you do pop into the gallery you must try their coffee and walnut cake, it's delicious.

When we were coming out, I saw a lovely painting. It was of two swans floating down a river. It had flowers, trees, grass and a beautiful blue sky with some fluffy white clouds. Lovely it were, and I told Bill that that was what made a good painting. He said I was a Phyllis Heine. I told him I was not a Phyllis Heine. That's the name of the floozy who stole My Jack from us.

He said he hadn't said Phyllis Heine, he said I was a Philistine! Now I'm not sure if it was meant as a compliment or an insult. Anyway, he's not talked to me since. But he'll come round. He always does 'cos he's a good lad.

Then there's Tom. Tom's married to Yvonne, another nice lady like Alice. Both Yvonne and Alice have a good sense of humour, well I guess they have to have, being married to my sons! Tom has two daughters and a son. Fiona, their eldest, is married with a baby and lives near Kendal. She's a lovely lass and her hubby's nice as well. Adam, Tom's youngest, is at university studying something quite useless. Philosophy! I mean what use is that in the real world? Will he be able to feed a family on philosophy? What sort of a job uses philosophy? I don't say anything, but it doesn't stop me thinking it! But he's a good lad for all that. The middle one, Artemis, a daft name if you ask me but then nobody did. Anyway, she's just got engaged and I was invited round for Sunday lunch to meet the guy. Malakai, another daft name if you ask me, but then nobody ever asks me! He's an odd looking person. He's well over six feet tall, thin as a lamppost, with black hair hanging down in a ponytail. He's got a goatee ginger beard, about eight inches long tapering to a point and curling under at the end, like he puts it in a hair roller at night. Most odd! Can you imagine it? Black boots, red trousers and a green shirt topped off with black hair and a ginger goatee! Like a giant blooming pixie he is!

All through the meal Artemis and Malakai were kissing and canoodling. Honest, it was too much! Even Adam told 'em. He said, 'I haven't come home to watch you two getting' it off. Get a room will ya!' I don't know what they were thinking of getting' off but the mind boggled. Well mine did anyway!

Yvonne made several pointed comments, but they ignored her. Tom just sat there with his head down ignoring 'em so I knew it was up to me to say something. I said, 'I was brought up to think that sex was like to going to the toilet. Something everyone did but not at the dinner table!' I thought Adam was going to choke on a roast spud, but it worked. As soon as they'd stopped giggling, they behaved!

When I come to think about it maybe Ruth's right. She has missed a lot by not having a family.

Darkness. Chill. Silence. Bliss
by Lesley Atherton

Summer isn't ice-cream and beaches. Not to me. The summer forces windows wide, admitting birdsong, creaking gates, the whirring of mowers, the madness of hedge trimmers, and the rhythmic cawing of noisy birds. Neighbourhood children add to this with shouts, as do their mothers, while the grinding, grating power tools add their white noise backing track.

The skies are bland and blue, adorned with swathes of dove-grey clouds. We wake early and retire late, and doze through the heat of the day, to be wakened by the *Greensleeves* of the ice cream van. Houses remain empty while and gardens fill with barbecue smoke and dogs.

But the darker months aren't all about the manic expectancy of Christmas, the craziness of shops, the worries of the poor and the extravagance of the rich. Winter brings its own silent, deafening beauty and the comforting sounds of rain and wind. The muggy blankness of the summer weather is a barrier to me, yet I'm drawn into winter's dramatic atmosphere. Tangible, dark and grey and as solid as my bed sheet. Winter rises late and snuggles down early in duvets that wrap us in their womblike comfort. The streets echo with cloistered emptiness.

In winter, there's a purposeful comfort in the orange glow of the light-bulbed room. You walk past a house and glance inside. You wonder about the lives within and are excited to arrive at your own glowing hobbit home.

I celebrate the differences of our seasonal extremes, but I know the one I like the best.

Winter's majesty, winter's peace and winter's rest are the introvert's perfect backdrop.

Winter's chill factor warms and energises my soul.

And autumn is a welcome transition.

Only five months more...

Going Home for Christmas
by David Jackson

I'm standing on the path outside the house. I've no idea how I got here.

There's snow falling, landing on my face and shoulders. Just a few flakes but it is snowing.

Maybe it's going to be a white Christmas this year. Can't remember the last one, can't remember a lot of things these days.

I remember being in the hospital, I remember the little room I had and the TV at the end of the bed with its awful reception, like seeing everything through a snowstorm. And the nurse, funny little fellow, Thai I think he said he was. And the food was awful. 'I'll be glad to get back to Mary's cooking,' I thought. Well here I am, but I haven't a clue how I got here.

They give you these memory tests at the hospital. Had one this morning. Well I think I did.

I rattled the answers off, easy.

'What's your name?' they ask, 'Can you tell me?'

And you say, 'Of course, it's Tom, Tom Churchward.'

'And what's your wife's name, your next of kin?'

'Mary, Mary Churchward'

'And when were you born?'

'That's easy, 3rd September 1939, my Dad said I'd always be able to remember that, it was the day war broke out.'

'So how old are you?'

'I'm seventy, three score years and ten.'

'What date is it?'

'It's Saturday, 24th December 2009,

'And who's the Prime Minister?'

'That Scots bloke, Gordon Brown. That enough for you? Look, am I going home for Christmas?'

'All in good time.'

See my memory's fine, but I don't remember the ride back here from the hospital at all.

Still better get inside, wonder why Mary didn't come to the hospital to collect me, she must be in the house. Hope she's not ill or anything.

I walk up the path. The front door's been painted, don't like that. Horrible green colour, she knows I don't like green. Maroon's the colour for a front door, there'll have to be words.

That's funny, front door's locked. I haven't a key in my pockets, I haven't anything in my pockets, and why am I wearing my best suit? I'll ring the bell.

No answer, I peer in through the windows, someone's been busy, all those Christmas decorations and the tree all decked out.

Where is Mary? I'll go round the back.

Veg beds have been turned over. Someone must have helped her while I've been in the hospital. That was kind. I'll try the back door.

It's locked too, I'll look through the window. She's had the kitchen done. Where's all this money come from? Has she won the bloody lottery? Why didn't she ask me about it? It's my house! And when did she get it done, they've been bloody quick.

Where is she? I'll try the church. Great churchgoer is Mary.

Of course, it's Christmas Eve, she'll probably be round there doing the flowers and the decorations, does it every year. Maybe they didn't tell her I was coming home, or maybe she just forgot. She wouldn't do that, surely?

I'm getting worried now, I hope she's OK. The vicar will know, it's that Reverend Marks now, young chap, all guitars and happy clappy stuff. Can't be doing with it myself, but Mary likes it. I preferred old Reverend Simmons, but he's gone now.

I walk out of the garden and down the back path to the church, though the churchyard and into the church itself.

'Hello, Tom,' says a voice, 'we've been waiting for you.'

It's Reverend Simmons, what's he doing here? And Mary's standing next to him smiling at me.

'What's going on, Mary?' I ask, 'I've been round the house, everything's been changed. How did it happen?'

'The house isn't ours anymore, Tom,' says Mary. 'Our Terry sold it about six months ago.'

'Our Terry, but he'd no right, how could...'

'What's the date, Tom?' interrupts Reverend Simmons.

'Not you too,' I sigh, 'it's Saturday 24th December

43

2009.'

    'Not quite,' says Simmons. 'It's Tuesday 24th December 2014. You've been gone 5 years, Tom.'

    '5 years, gone, gone where, what do you mean?'

    'I'll explain it all later,' Mary says, 'but now we have to get on our way. Come along Tom.'

    And Mary leads the way out through a side door of the church I've never used before, and into the churchyard. We go down the path towards the back fence.

    'Something else new,' I think, 'there's never been a gate here before.'

    But Reverend Simmons opens the gate and beckons us through.

    As I move towards the gate, I notice two newish gravestones one on each side of the path. The first says 'In memory of Reverend Brian Simmons, vicar of this parish 1980 – 2008, died April 10th 2014, aged 90 years' and the other has two inscriptions 'In Memory of Thomas Churchward, born 3rd September 1939, died December 24th 2009' and 'Also his wife, Mary Churchward, born 5th June 1945, died November 24th 2014'. There are fresh flowers on the second grave.

Father's Greatcoat
by Malcolm Timms

The night it had fallen, the cold would be hell.
It would get much colder we both knew it well.
As my brother and I huddled closer together,
This old council house wasn't built for this weather.

The heating was basic and coal and coke dear,
Of a roaring fire in this house, there would be no fear.
We'd plenty of blankets, of wool and horse hair.
There were six in this house, we all had to share.

My elder brothers were lucky as they all well knew,
Their bedroom was warmed by the scullery flue.
'Don't worry my pets,' mother said from the door.
'Dad will be home soon, of that I'm quite sure.'

Dad was a bus driver and on such a night,
His bus, warm and cosy, was a welcoming sight.
To revellers, workers, the cold huddled masses,
Even night students going home from their classes.

And then we heard the familiar sound of his bike
Proclaiming the arrival of this family's knight.
The backdoor was closed, the lock it was thrown
The world's greatest bus driver had come safely home.

The tread on the stairs heralded our saviour's arrival
To banish this cold, give us chance for survival,
His greatcoat he flourished like Raleigh's old cloak
The warmth provided our bodies would soak.

Across the bed, like an almighty black wave,
From the stabbing ice lances our bodies to save.
A kiss on our foreheads, a cheeky old grin
The chill now abated our slumbers begin.

First Footing
by Neville Southern

There's a cold wind blowing,
An icy rime on winter landscape.
First footing in the dark of the New Year
Brings the promise of hope reborn.
Spring will come when, in due time,
Frost and snow will melt.

I will stand at the window
Watching the snow melt
As quickly as it falls, and will know
That love is spreading in the snow.
Though I cannot see it, it will be there,
Promising a summer's bounty.

Like Nature, I must reflect and take stock,
Marshall all my resourced, consider
Where effort should best be directed,
To aim for achievement.
The long, slow business of learning how to live
Begins again as the New Year turns homeward.

The First Time I Went Potholing
by Roy Bennett

The first time I was invited to go underground, it was an individual thing. There were no potholing clubs and basically most of Britain's potholes were just holes in the ground not many people had explored.

Being an outgoing sort of a chap, I was invited to a meeting of four or five gents who had a likewise curiosity about where the water coming out of the ground came from and went to.

There is an area of Yorkshire known as the Pavements or the Clint's, where the glaciers had cleared the debris and left a flat track over the terrain. Over time the frosts had formed cracks in the rock and water had dissolved the soft limestone into the strange shapes we see today.

Some of these holes and fissures were quite deep and elicited a discussion amongst us about what and where they went and what would be needed to explore these caves and potholes. They give their presence away by deep dips in the moors, called shake-holes, which were part of the cave system.

The equipment we started off with consisted of strong cotton ropes, a bowler hat, 3 candles, two boxes of matches dipped in wax, a one-piece woollen undergarment (rather like the ones John Wayne used to wear in his cowboy films.) some underpants, strong boots and a pair of overalls. That was the initial equipment we used.

A lot of potholes had never been explored, and there were many as yet undiscovered, so it was a challenge and an adventure.

Each of us had to look after the safety of the person in front of them and behind them. Because we were going into the unknown, we had to have a code for survival.

Excitement grew as we decided which potholes, we would go in. It was decided to explore the ones that had water coming out as opposed to going in, - as it was evidence of a natural drainage. We figured the water would help to push us out if we needed to exit quickly. Some pots flooded within twenty minutes when it rained so we also had to be aware of the weather conditions. Not having experienced potholing before the excitement was high. The common idea that a pothole is a dark gloomy place is a fallacy. Even by candlelight you have your own sphere of illumination. We could see some four to six feet ahead, depending on the formation we were in.

The first cave we tried was called Skerwith. It is about two miles from White scar, further down toward Ingleton. It was a cold frosty day with a thin smattering of snow on the ground. On getting there, we sorted out the equipment we knew we needed. We put plenty of wax on the brim of our bowler hats so that a candle could be perched on it – then one by one we dropped in, down a knotted rope. We secured the rope to a boulder, all too aware that this was our only known exit.

On arriving at the bottom of the rope we found ourselves in a chamber -that is; a wide space in a cave created by water. The thought that we were the first to stand in such a place was exhilarating. Further on down the passage, water had worn a small cascade which went down into a hole. We threw a rock into it and listening, we assessed how deep the hole was. Having concluded it was not too far down for the rope available, one of us went over the edge tied to the rope and disappeared from sight – the water having put out the candle. The only indication that he had reached the bottom safely was a tug on the rope and then there was an effort of his to light the candle and that gave us a glimpse of the depth. Part of the excitement was finding that at the bottom, there was another chamber in which he was able to relight the candle. There was a pool of light to show us that there was something we were able to stand on. It was the next chapter of our descent

To stand in a place like that was like being at the bottom of an ice cream cone. Everywhere was white and glistening. As above, so below. There were strange formations; curtains, stalactites and stalagmites. Some had joined together to make pillars. They had taken eons in creation. In some chambers there were fine rods from floor to ceiling that shattered as we spoke. Our voices were the first vibrations for millennia. The beauty of it all, in soft candlelight, never ceased to amaze me. We were the first to see this.

Now a sobering thought. What has gone down had to get back up. In these days, photography was difficult in such circumstances. There were no electronic flashlights. We had to take a tin of magnesium powder, open the shutters of the camera, focus on what you wanted to take a picture of, and then you put the candles out and were in total darkness. A darkness so cloying you could feel it like black velvet. Then some brave person had to poke a match into the flash powder. The secret was to blink as the flash went off otherwise, even with candlelight, you could not see much. The flash was utterly blinding. But in the candlelight everything took on a life of its own. The brilliance seemed to be absorbed into the whiteness of the walls and for about half a minute it lingered, then utter darkness again until someone got a fresh candle out from under their hat and using waxed matches, coaxed it back to life.

Having explored to see how far the passage extended our adventure underground was governed by the length of time the candles lasted. We agreed that when we were halfway down the last candle, we would return the way we came.

This was the beginning of my enthusiasm for the beauty of underground Britain.

Guzzunder
by Malcolm Timms

Under the bed, your gleaming whiteness has now turned pale,
Filled to the brim with what was last night's ale.
A vision from my childhood I cannot elude,
Looking back, it now seems oh so crude.
And yet there may be rhyme and reason
Long ago in a cold winter season,
A time when the outer portal was not there
And our downstairs loo was not a place you could bear.
Beyond the back door, neither safe nor sound.
A Bakelite seat, the chill was profound.
Now I can see why it might be so respectable,
To have this portable urine receptacle.
As I lay here at 4 am, sleep would be bliss.
Oh bugger it, now I must go for a piss.

Heads You Lose
by Sally James

Jack wandered in and out of the back yard watching his dad as he fiddled with his rusty old bike then giggled when he saw him throw the spanner into the air. It landed with a splutter onto the already cracked flags.

His dad never had the best of patience and was easily provoked so when he saw Jack laughing, he threw it. He never could help these outbursts of annoyance. The spanner missed Jack's head by a whisker and sent him scampering down the alley and to the street where his mates lingered.

Some were kicking a ball, a battered one that had seen better days and a few lads were smoking fag ends they had found in the gutter.

The light of a street lamp yellowed their faces, made them look twice their age and a stray dog cocked its leg against the cast iron base.

'What's up?' a scrawny lad said, his eyes narrowing as he inhaled a lungful of nicotine.

'Nowt just mi dad actin' up agen.' Jack smirked holding his hand out for a drag.

'Careful ah've only got that one.'

'Awreet then just a little un an then am gooin whoam.' Jack replied taking a few puffs from a soggy Woodbine.

It began to snow as he walked back home, he kicked a stray cat in his way, pulled his collar up to his eyes then hurried past his house when he heard his father shout and his mother cry.

Jack was used to this on a Friday night when his dad came home the worse for wear but not now on Monday evening when it was only just dark.

He went back down the alley to sneak in the back way. With any luck he could be up the stairs and in his room in a flash. The lads had gone but the stray dog was still there sniffing. A gentle splattering of snow dusted the cobbles and the clogs Jack wore were silenced.

As Jack crept through the back gate, he noticed his dad's bike still in bits in the yard, his mother was at the kitchen sink peeling potatoes. There was no sign of his dad.

'Tha's gone an done it neaw lad,' his mother chastised. Her eyes were red, and Jack thought he saw the birth of a bruise on her cheek, but he said nothing only, 'Sorry mam'. He could never stand seeing his mother upset.

'He needs his bike fer work tha knows, that's why he gets all peevish, tha shouldn't a goaded him, it doesn't tek much tha knows.'

She sighed and nodded to him "e's gone t'th bike shop but ah'll bet it's shut neaw so we'd better watch eawt when he com's back whoam.'

Jack had a bright idea. He was only ten years old, but he reckoned he could fix his dad's bike. He had often watched the big lads mending punctures and putting chains back on, he knew he could do it. When his mother had finished in the kitchen, he fetched the bike and bits and pieces from the yard and laid them all out on newspaper.

It didn't take him long, he mended the puncture, got the tyre back on the wheel frame and oiled all the moving parts. He was just tightening up the brakes when his dad walked through the front door.

Instead of looking angry because the shop had closed, Jack noticed how sad and dejected he looked, his black shadowed eyes showing the onset of weariness.

'Well that's it,' he murmured, 'a corn't get in fer work in't' mornin' so that's that',

He held out his arms to his wife. 'Sorry lass' and again 'Sorry lass'.

It had always been like that, his dad losing his temper, his mother whimpering and then the making up, snuggling together on the old armchair.

'What do'st want neaw?' his dad sighed as his son walked into the living room.

'A've mended thi bike dad, 'ere tek a look.'

'Tha cornt 'ave, 'ah've bin strugglin' aw afternoon sin' a com' whoam fro't' pit.'

'Well 'a've done it 'a've mended it, see fer thi sel',' Jack beckoned

His dad crept from the chair reluctant now to leave the comfort of his wife's arms and went into the kitchen. He couldn't believe his eyes, not only was the bike in one piece but it was clean and shiny.

'That's good lad, tha's done a good job, but does it wark?' he queried.

'Aye, 'course it will, go on 'ave a go.'. Jack's wide beaming smile showed his pride at a job well done.

His dad tried the bike out in the back yard, tested the brakes and the tyre pressures and found even the rusty old bell now rang with a jolly tinkle.

'Eeh lad tha's done a good job, ah'm grateful toh thi, 'ere 'ave this, ah wer' savin' it fer a special occasion.'

He reached for a battered old tea caddy on top of the mantelpiece and shook a shiny new penny on to the kitchen table; it rolled around and glittered in the gaslight before finally coming to a halt head uppermost.

'Thanks dad.' Jack's smile went broader and even more so when he felt his dad's arms around his shoulder.

They were never a family for showing much affection to their offspring so this was a grand gesture on his dad's behalf.

Jack never forgot this. All his life he remembered the strong arm around his shoulder, the bright new penny twirling around on the kitchen table and the way the gaslight made it glimmer as if it was pure gold

Jack went up to his bedroom, his warm feet pattering on the cold linoleum, his newly scrubbed hands clutching the bright new penny.

He curled next to his younger brother who was warm and soft and smelled of soap and newly washed hair.

He slept contentedly all night, the penny tucked safely under his pillow; his arm wrapped around his brother, their combined breath making lacy patterns on the windowpane.

That was the last time Jack ever saw his dad, but he did hear him the following morning, wheeling the bike out of the kitchen, the snap and click of the back door, the creak of the gate and his whistle as he cycled down the back alley and into the street.

When he got home from school his mother was crying, the fire had died down in the grate and she was cold and trembling. The house seemed strangely bare.

A neighbour took him to her house gave him some tea; it was kippers with tiny bones that tickled his throat. He never liked kippers after that day.

Then his mother came for him with his two aunties, May and Renee who lived three streets away. When he saw them, he knew it was trouble as he only ever saw them at funerals wearing tiny black hats with big feathers.

The funeral was on a Wednesday afternoon, it was the day they had the maths test and Archie Slater slipped on the ice and banged his head on the school railings.

He pleaded to go to see his dad laid to rest, so his mother gave in. Funerals were not places for children, she always said, but from then on he would be the man of the house and would have to grow up fast.

The church service passed in a blur except for the words about a blast down the pit, an escape of gas, how his father had been caught in the middle along with two others.

All this happened many years ago and Jack still has that penny, a little duller now, wrapped in a piece of his dad's shirt inside his old tobacco tin.

His mother never really got over her husband's death, but like most pit wives she bore it well. Jack had a new brother soon after and she called him Tommy after his dad,

Life went on as life has to, but she wouldn't have her sons going down the pit, so she took in washing, baked wedding and Christmas cakes and Jack got a few coppers every week for mending things.

'Aye he can fettle anythin',' his mother would say.

Jack and his brothers did well and though there was little work outside the pit in that area of Lancashire they managed to find something suitable.

Time passes as time does and things alter as they do. One by one the pits closed in Lancashire and there was nothing left to be seen, no pit head gears, no slag heaps, nothing to remind people of the harsh reality of those days.

But in a little bungalow on the outskirts of Wigan, an old man sits by a gas fire, tosses a penny into the air, watches it spin and dance on a polished top table, glint in the light and rest face uppermost.

Happy New Year
by Delia Southern

The old woman standing by the kerb saw that the passing car was about to splash her, and tried to step back, but she caught her heel and sat down just as the dirty, icy water arced across the pavement. The car stopped and a young man dashed back towards Janice, who was trying, without success, to get to her feet.

'I'm so sorry, I couldn't swerve, or I would have crashed into the bus. Are you hurt? Sorry, silly thing to say. Of course you are. And your coat is soaked and covered in mud. Can I take you home? Or do you need the hospital? What can I do?'

All this fuss was flustering Janice, who just wanted to be left alone to recover. She was more embarrassed than hurt, because she had landed in a small, muddy flowerbed, not on concrete. More people were gathering, too. One of them was Anne, a volunteer at the Age UK shop, who knew Janice, a regular customer.

Anne pulled Janice to her feet and put an arm round her. 'I'll take her into my shop, just there; she can sit quietly and have a cup of tea. What you could do, if you want to help, is pay for her coat to be cleaned.'

Relieved, the young man stuffed something into Janice's pocket, apologised again and rapidly took himself off.

Anne took Janice into the back room of the shop, removed her muddy coat, sat her down in a battered but comfortable chair, and put the kettle on to boil.

'You can't go our again like this. We can look what we have that will fit you and you can borrow it and bring it back tomorrow.'

While Janice drank her tea in peace, Anne went into the shop. She came back with a hooded mac with a thick, quilted lining. 'This will get you home both dry and warm. Try it on for me, love.'

Picking up the old muddy coat, she emptied the pockets onto the table. Purse, hanky, bus pass, plastic bag, keys and a small roll of notes.

'Janice, is this everything you should have? Check it, please.'

'Those notes aren't mine.'

Anne unrolled the notes. 'There's a hundred pounds here! Well! We don't know how to get hold of him. We just have to accept that he knew what he was giving you. What do you want to do with it?'

'I can have the warm waterproof mac; I can have shoes and an umbrella. Oh, Anne, thanks for your help. Thanks to the young man, too. How kind you both are. What a morning. Happy New Year indeed!'

Joe's Story
by Sally James

Joe pulled the collar of his army overcoat to just above the tips of his earlobes. He scowled, a wet whiskery scowl as floating snowflakes danced into his narrowed eyes, then melted upon his bedraggled moustache which drooped with steamed breath and slivers of bacon fat.

He shuffled, his burdened feet encased in boots two sizes too big and lined with pages from the last weeks newspaper. He left a heavy trail behind him in the drifting snow as he gasped and wheezed his way past the boiler house of the local paper mill. 'Nearly whoam neaw,' he blew, like a train steaming to a halt.

Home to Joe was his best kept secret and no one knew where he disappeared to on cold winter afternoons like this one and nobody cared for that matter. His usual haunts were already overflowing with the debris of society, and no one had the slightest inclination to follow a shuffling, grumpy, old man, though Joe didn't see himself like that at all.

Over the stile, then down the railway embankment he almost tumbled in his haste, under the archway were the river sped furiously, overlapping the stone slabs, yet never daring to enter Joe's sanctuary, now overgrown with weeds and clumps of dead grass.

Once inside the tunnel, he half crawled, until he reached the part where he could stand comfortably, the river ebbing and sobbing as it echoed and meandered in the damp gloom. It was barely light, but Joe knew instinctively where he was heading. The feeble light from the match he held shakily, guided his narrowed eyes to a hole in the wall of the tunnel. The gap was just big enough for Joe to crawl inside, his gnarled, arthritic fingers, groping root-like in the damp earth as he felt for his torch.

'That's better,' he sighed, glad to be in his home for the night. The light from his torch automatically seeking out his army blanket sleeping bag, his crackling sheets of polythene, whisky bottle candle sticks and half bottle of navy rum, which protruded, unashamedly from a gap in the wall. He treasured this

place, his sanctuary, it was dry and warm inside the divide
between the wall of the river tunnel and the stone, mill wall. The
warmth from the nearby boiler house filtered in through the old
brickwork and the cracks in the stonework made instant central
heating.

He would bed down for the night, sip his rum by
candlelight till the last train screamed overhead at ten and the
factory whistle blew at six. Whatever was going on in the cold
world outside and above he did not care to know, only the river
gurgling and splashing its way beneath the streets shared Joe's
secret life below ground and water did not talk.

It was at times like this that Joe would reminisce, think
of better and happier times, though snug and warm with his
bottle of rum under his overcoat pillow, Joe thought he could not
have been happier. But he knew deep down that this was far
from the truth, he did have a life before being homeless,
unemployed, forgotten.

Once upon a time he was a cherished child, with no
other ambition than to follow in the footsteps of his father and
like his father before him, he would become a miner, a hard nut,
a salt of earth rough, tough, Lancashire miner.

Sliding down the slag heaps, ripping his short trousers
in the process, he would come home after a hard days play, just
as black as if he had done a shift down the pit, that's what his
mother would say as she scrubbed his father's back with red
carbolic soap. Then laughing, would chase the young Joe around
the kitchen table, grab him by his tattered jumper, peel off his
ragged clothes, and make him dive for cover in the dregs of his
father's bath water.

Two naked males in the tin bath, in front of the kitchen
fire and his mother never batted an eye lid, just scrubbed like
there was no tomorrow, all the time singing in her soft accent the
popular tunes of the day.

There was a war on, the country needed coal and it was
the likes of Joe's father who supplied it and Joe thought he
would do the same.

'Ger er job in't pit lad un thall have gor er job for life, if
tha con stond it thar is, money's not bad either tha knows, un tha
can ger er coal board house when tha marries, aye, er lass ull not
go fer rung if er marries er pit mon.'

Well at least that's what the people in Joe's village said, and so that seemed to be the case until 1985.

Margaret Thatcher's government came out with their plan for coal.

All unprofitable pits were to close, there would be no more subsidies, coal would be replaced by other fuels, there was North Sea oil now and Nuclear Power. Coal it seems would become obsolete, old communities and ways of life were going to be destroyed. The instinct in that small community became to fight for survival.

Joe new straight away what he had to do and that a difficult task lay ahead. His dad was too old and too ill to work underground he was just another retired miner with a lung full of slack to cough up, but it didn't stop him going on picket duty. He had to fight for his heritage and for his son's right to work, and like the Luddites and the Tollpuddle Martyrs before them, father and son vowed to fight to the bitter end.

Joe fought hard and long in that bitter strike with his father and mates alongside him, trying to convince the scabs and to maintain order on the picket line. One of Scargill's men Joe was, a union man, a do or die man.

'Sod Thatcher and her hench man, McGreggor,' he would argue. 'Sod the Tories with their plan for coal, what about us poor buggers when all them mines are shut, there's plenty er coal down theer, enough to see me and our kids in employment for a hundred years.'

When all the shouting and arguing and fighting was over, it was Joe and his kind who came the worst off, they couldn't win they were beaten before they even started. He fought and lost, lost his job, his house, the lot, what hadn't been sold for food his wife took when she left with their two young sons to live with some fancy man she had met when staying with friends in the South.

Life for Joe became tougher than ever, after giving his wife a share of his redundancy money, he idled about, spent his money on booze and the dogs, he could not get going again. Thatcher had not only broken up the unions, she had broken up communities and people's spirits, some did survive, moved on but without his family Joe felt he had nothing to live for.

When they placed his father's body alongside his mother's in the moorland cemetery, he felt his life was over. He could see them in the past and he could see them in the present, he smiled in the flickering candle light, as he pictured his mother, eternally scrubbing his father's back and singing, 'Cruising down the river on a Sunday afternoon,' and 'I'd like to get you on a slow boat to China'.

They were on a slow boat to China alright now, he almost choked as he swallowed a mouthful of the hard, pungent, rum.

He went back to the village once, just to make sure his life before had not been a dream or even a nightmare for that matter, but it may have well have been, for there was nothing left of the old pit, except for the pit head wheel, which had been salvaged for a children's playground.

In the dank, misty morning, the old iron wheel turned, gaily painted in bright primary colours, a spinning wheel of fortune or a magical mystery ride, with Joe clinging on desperately, with clenched fists and grim determination. His boots, dangling dangerously, skimming the black puddles.

Wide eyed children stared in amazement as the tramp sped in ever decreasing circles until it finally came to a staggered halt. 'Come away,' a woman shrieked in protective instinct to the two little boys who eyed him with awe. 'He looks like a strange man to me,' she snapped, dragging them into a house.

Joe did the honours and left, he was not wanted, even in his own village, which bore no resemblance to the village he knew in his early life. No slag heaps loomed dark and foreboding, dominating the village with underground waste, the only industry he had ever known had been wiped off the face of his earth forever.

'And for what?' he questioned. 'Was it to get rid of the shame of men crawling like worms on their bellies for generations? Why?' he almost screamed in bitterness, 'were my memories, dreams, obliterated, wiped clean, like shit of a boot, with nor even a placard, just derelict wasteland waiting to be reclaimed?'

He felt rage rising inside him like an animal trapped, at the thought of a century of men being used and abused for commercial gain. He thought of the huge gaps in the earth beneath his feet, a place where men lived and worked. Broken, he slouched heavily, cursing to himself, as he tramped his weary way down the street that he once lived in. Where his mother scrubbed, where his sons like he did long ago, fought and dreamed and played in the narrow lanes, where blackberry bushes grabbed at unsuspecting young ankles. Where streams turned into raging torrents in winter and were frog spawn floated in nanny green teeth water in spring.

There was nothing left now but an eerie stillness, save for the distant yapping of whippets and the cooing of pigeons as they flew home to roost.

Yet there were some reminders that life had been something more concrete, more than just a fading memory, a dream. The video shop which now sold everything, the only thriving business in an area of absence, where a family of Asians wished him well and gave him a glass of water and said how business had been bad since the pit had closed and how the village was not the same any more. The launderette next to it, steam and fabric softener mingling with the morning mist, and surprisingly the bookies office, were a couple of men coughed and spluttered inside to place their bets and he wondered after all these years if he would recognize them.

His house, belonging to the coal board, now long neglected, had been boarded up and lay derelict and deserted. Shutters hammered in the morning breeze as if to say, 'let me in'. Joe made his way inside and decided to spend the night there, scour the crumbling house for the man he once was, but instead he spent a restless, haunted, night. There was nothing left to salvage, only the foul smell of decay remained, and the remnants of an era long gone.

He left before dawn the next day, back to the warmth of the town, where the mist mingled with the neon lights and welcomed him with curled, smoky fingers. He did this well before anyone could catch sight of him scurrying like a rat along the disused pathways and byways, back to his dwelling by the river.

'And me,' he almost sobbed like the river winding and twisting in his underworld, 'this is what's happened toh me.'

'Forgotten, deserted, like mi owd house, stuck here, in a

hole, in a wall, in't dark, wi only th' river for company an' th' hissin ert steam, un this,' he said holding up the bottle of rum but the rumbling of the ten o'clock train distracted him. He shook his head, and sobbed, and drank his fill, and laid his head down to rest, the candles, flickering and rattling with the vibrations from the last train, which sped onwards, in the still blackness of the night.

Then it happened, those once in a lifetime experiences, when time stands still, and old mens' hearts, twist and turn like closed fists within the chest. His breath strangled in his throat, yet he felt the energy to run, his boots echoing down the tunnel, sparking like the candle he clenched so firmly.

Flapping like a huge bird in flight his overcoat wings seemed to soar as he sped towards the faint light at the end of the tunnel. His breath burning in his throat, till the ache inside him became like a hunger for freedom and light. Reaching the snow blocked mouth of the tunnel, he scratched and clawed his way to escape, till the black night sky, star sparkling, welcomed him.

He snorted the sharp, still air till the beat of his heart fell once more into a regular rhythm pattern, and lay there in the silent snow, half in and half out of the tunnel.

When he awoke, it was to a warm bed and unfamiliar faces. He was attached by wires to machines and a mask framed his face were his whiskers usually were.

'Hello. Welcome to the world, dad.'

Disorientated, Joe tried to speak, as he did so, a nurse darted forward and removed the tube from his mouth.

'He will be alright now,' she murmured softly to the fair haired young man, 'but please don't tire him'.

Joe had woken to a new life though he did not know it at the time. Those next few days were to become the happiest and most memorable of his life. He learned that he had been found by a young boy on his way to do his paper round. Only the skill of the doctors and nurses had saved him. Now sitting up clean and fresh he looked almost distinguished, his beard and hair had been trimmed to a reasonable length, he smelled much sweeter and an old familiar smile ironed out his wrinkles

He learned he had suffered a heart attack and survived freezing temperatures, drifting in and out of consciousness for days. The rum, the doctors had said had aided his survival. His

wife and sons had recognized him only by the crumpled
wedding photo that he kept in his overcoat pocket and which had
been circulated to the local newspapers. Joe it seemed had only
lived within a ten mile radius of them for many years.

Over the next few weeks, Joe learned a lot about the
reality he had shunned for over a decade. His wife had returned
home after a few months only to find Joe had gone and since
then, along with their two sons, had tried desperately to find
him. Over the years they never gave up hope that one day they
would be reconciled. The sons were doing well, both at
University and both with good prospects ahead of them.

When Molly, his wife, had realized her mistake she had
returned to her mother's home broken hearted and spent her
share of his redundancy money on their education.

'You see dad,' the young lad said, gazing straight into
his father's eyes. 'Mam never wanted us down the pit, like you
and your dad, and her dad too for that matter.'

'She wanted us to make something of ourselves.'

'We've broken the chain, dad.'

'Let coal stay dead and buried. Anything's better than
crawling like a worm all your life to earn a living.'

Seeing his sons before him, bright and eager eyed, their
fair unblemished skin, without a trace of coal dust and looking
forward to a future before them, Joe smiled a sad smile.

'Eh lads,' he said at last a faraway look in his bright
blue eyes 'Aye, tha's probably reet, seeing yor two in front er
me, makes me think, perhaps it's time I looked forard instead er
backards.'

'Nobody will ever forget what you and your kind did
dad.'

'We won't let them dad.'

'I know tha won't lads, dost think have bin an owd
foo.'

'You did what you thought was right at the time.'

'We'll look after you now dad as well as mam.'

'Come on, it's time we got our act together. We've a lot
of catching up to do.'

As each lad hugged their father, they could not help but
notice the tears that trickled like a river down his cheeks and
lodged in the remains of his beard.

'Dost think have bin given er second chance, lads, time this owd worm turned once un fer all?' he questioned quietly, as he held Molly's hand in his grip and her lips gently brushed his tears away.

Lancashire Legacy
by Sally James

I look out of the window, see the snow on the hills, my bed is warm, the duvet tucked under my chin, a cup of hot tea on the bedside cabinet and a book begging to be read. I will stay here where it is comfortable. I decide no need to get up, for I am too old, past it and happy.

My mind wanders as I look over the distant moors and think of those early days when I first came to live in a certain cotton town in Lancashire. I wasn't in a hurry to get up in those days either. I was young with a baby on the way, the window iced up in the sparse bedroom and the linoleum cold to my bare feet.

We had nothing you see, less than nothing, a friend once said, 'Som' foak start at t' bottom ut t'ladder but thee two need a brick toh ger on t'bottom step'. And so it was with many folk in those days. We were barely out of our teens, married and with a baby on the way. It may have been the 'Swinging Sixties' in London but here in Lancashire nothing swung except perhaps the washing on the line.

Every other day I would go into town to see if there were any houses to rent. It was like 'No room at the Inn' wherever you went. There was a very long waiting list for a council house and so it came to be that we lived with the in-laws until we could find a place of our own.

This was the winter of 1962-63 and the coldest winter on record since 1947. I did have the baby to keep me warm in his snug little nest in my tummy though chilblains bothered my toes but with an army overcoat thrown over the bed to hold the heat in, we managed.

The baby came in the middle of March, a cold blustery day when ice and snow still tinged the distant moors. With no pram till the baby was a couple of weeks old I couldn't go out and was desperate to show off my new baby. Then a relative, who had promised us a pram, sold us one for £5 but as my husband's weekly wage was £8 it wasn't much of a bargain for a third hand pram, but it was a good one and we knew its heritage, so we made do.

Eventually after trekking into town plus baby and pram nearly every day for almost two months we got somewhere to live. It was a mid-terraced house on a cobbled street in the heart of industrial Lancashire. With mills to the left of us and mills to the right of us and in front of us the weaving shed of a large cotton mill whose looms rattled and clanged twenty four hours a day five and a half days a week. Sunday was maintenance day when the looms were silent, so silent that I could hear the church bells ring.

'Tha'll get used toh noise,' I was told but I never did. I liked peace and quiet but everywhere there was hustle and bustle. People clogging their way to work at six o'clock in the morning, and then coming back at two o'clock in the afternoon as another batch of factory fodder went to replace them. Yet they were cheerful happy souls and as I pushed my pram on the stone flags and cobbles there was always a cheery smile to greet you with a 'Heaw do'. In fact, the first words my baby said were 'Heaw do'.

I got our little love nest as comfy as I could with the money we had saved, for there was no living off the bank of mum and dad in those days. We bought a few items of furniture that we could just about afford. The bed was a divan, quite posh really as we were used to an iron framed one with flock bedding that had to be kneaded every morning before making up. We also managed a kitchenette, a Formica topped table and four kitchen chairs and even a green moquette three piece suite on the never never. We did get a small electric cooker too which was paid monthly via the electricity bill. It seemed like we were doing ok but the first morning for breakfast I realised there were no plates so with great laughter I ate Weetabix from a frying pan.

There were five jars in the bedroom marked, rent, coal, electric, insurance, and the never never jar. When these were budgeted for what remained was spent on food. There was nothing left for luxuries like clothes, so I knitted, sewed, darned, made do and mended. Bury Market remnant stall was a Godsend for me. 1964 saw me pushing and shoving the huge pram from Elton to Bury market, with the hopes of getting a bargain or two.

That pram became a vehicle of transport for not only a couple of babies for by 1964 I had two but also going to the Laundrette with a plastic bag full of clothes and bedding as we had no washer. It was also used for collecting groceries and vegetables from Bury Market probably a four mile journey there and back. There were no supermarkets in those days.

For eighteen months we lived in our first home amidst the smoke from mill chimneys and steam trains that chuffed their way over a bridge only a couple of hundred yards from the end of the street. With not much sun to penetrate the gloom, the shadows of industrialisation swamped us, but we were not discouraged. Even when a new influx of labour arrived to work in the mills from India and Pakistan we didn't mind, though they did look poor and undernourished as some walked around with blankets around them after work. It was years later that I was told that they had only one or two sets of working clothes between them so as one finished at the mill the other changed into their clothes for the next shift.

Oh dear, why do I day-dream, reminisce, it makes me feel sad, but we never did feel sorry for ourselves in those days or considered ourselves hard done by, we never even felt that life had dealt us a raw deal.

'Thas med tha bed so tha mun lie in it,' is what I was told and so I dealt with it. We had youth and health on our side and were happy despite my intense dislike of scrubbing nappies in the sink or slop-stone as it was called in those days. We had just cold water on tap, so I boiled the nappies in a large pan on the stove. There were no disposable nappies in those days.

I look at my hands now, they are wrinkled concertina fashion with blue veins throbbing as I hold my teacup in my hand. They are soft gentle hands now but in my young days my fingers would be cracked with scrubbing and chapped with the winter wind when I pegged the nappies out on the clothesline in the backyard.

I must get up, no more reminiscing but my bed is warm, my aching limbs resting, and I can see the sun rising a little higher over the hilltops. It is January with sporadic dustings of snow in the garden and on the car. There were not many cars in those days or indeed could be afforded by ordinary working people, so my husband went to work on his bike. He worked in a paper-mill about four miles away but never complained even if he got soaked and the smog clogged his nostrils. I look towards were he should have been lying, there is no sag in the pillow where his head would have lain, he has gone now, the strain of working twelve hour shifts in a paper-mill may have contributed to his early demise.

Yes, now I am getting maudlin, I had better get up for my son will be calling with his family and strangely enough he now works in the same street that I used to walk along many years ago. There is a huge depot there now, a sorting office for parcels and mail, where there once was a busy working mill. This depot is where my son works, the cobbled street now tarmacked was where his father rode his bike and I pushed my pram, babies, washing and all but that was over fifty years ago.

There is still one mill left standing not quite derelict and this has been turned into units for various occupations and where my eldest grandson has a recording studio. The weaving shed has long since gone as is the railway bridge and chimneys and so is the house we lived in, there is no sound of marching clogs, factory whistles or the chuffing trains anymore but in my mind it is as clear as yesterday.

I live in a different part of Lancashire now where I can see the hills and moor land and smell the earth instead of the soot and smog of Lancashire's industrial heritage. I can never erase those early days and wouldn't want to, for it is ingrained in me forever for I, like many things in those days was made in Lancashire.

Last Christmas
by Eva Martindale

...I gave you my heart. Committed, and with total optimism for the future, that is what I did. I lie in bed awake now listening to the central heating purring and my exposed toe tells me not to get up just yet. I reach across for my phone to see the time, across that cold half of the bed that was yours and which I can still not bring myself to sleep in. Too early to rise, even though it is Christmas Day. Normally we would be up by now, acting like children and rushing downstairs. I would switch the tree lights on and find the cd of the Westminster Boys Choir singing Christmas carols while you make a pot of coffee, then in perfect synchronisation we would settle ourselves and start the present opening. Lots of 'oohs' and 'ahs', even though I already knew what I was getting. I don't know what normal is anymore. You hate mess and would gather up all the paper and ribbon as soon as possible whilst I would gather up the TV times and turn the page. My programmes marked in red, yours in black and a timetable by which to set the other events of the day.

Your prize possession is your bicycle, and cycling your passion, so you always go for a bike ride with your 2 friends who feel just the same about their machines, whilst I would install the Kindle, or whatever gadget I had selected that year, and work out the best time to peel the sprouts and potatoes so that I would be free to watch Morecambe & Wise, glass of Bailys in hand. It never really worked out that way because there would be something far more important on that you needed to watch, so the bottle of Baileys stayed in the kitchen with me whilst I carried on preparing the festive feast. And what a feast indeed! Turkey crown, roasted to perfection with crispy skin – just how you like it – potatoes boiled then coated in semolina before being roasted in goose fat, masses of sprouts – you love them- carrots, peas, roast parsnips, Tesco finest pigs in blankets, cranberry sauce, and homemade gravy and stuffing. It would take me hours to prepare but I was proud of the result and the table looked like a page from Good Housekeeping with the polished glasses and cutlery and masses of decorations. Then we would sit down, pull crackers, don the paper hats from inside and eat the meal. 20 minutes later you would be back in front of the tv, having muttered that you would clear the table when there was nothing on tv, and I would look at the remains of my hard work. And Christmas was actually hard work – hard work pretending to be enjoying the ancient ritual with somebody I had no feelings for and who felt nothing for me in return. I hated the Westminster Boys Choir and the reason I knew what I was getting as a present was because you would always tell me to 'go and buy it and I'll give you the money so I don't get the wrong one', knowing all along that it was really because you couldn't be bothered. As much as I planned to watch Morecambe & Wise, or anything else marked in red, I knew well beforehand that marking programmes was a futile exercise, because you would mock my suggestion and I would pretend not to hear the huff and puff when you had to leave the tv to come and eat.

So today I will not have to peel those horrible sprouts or wash the muddy sweaty lycra after your bike ride, nor will I have to rummage through the bin to pull out a bath bomb that you gathered up in your haste to rid the lounge of paper. I will definitely be watching Morecambe & Wise, bottle of Baileys at my side, next to the TV times that has no markings because I will channel hop all day and miss nothing. My M&S meal for one has everything I wish for and is devoid of sprouts. I will pop it in the oven during some adverts. Then it's off to the pub to meet all of my family – you know the ones you never got on with. With these warm thoughts I turn over in bed to feel you at the side of me and the warmth turns to a chill. We do not always get what we wish for. Maybe I will have the courage to leave before next Christmas.

The Late Father Christmas
by Lynne Taylor

Chief Inspector Cavendish had attended many murder scenes, but none as surreal as this. The room was black and white, the only exception being the frozen turkey and the blood red body lying on the black hearthrug.

'What can you tell me Sergeant?' asked the Chief Inspector.

Before Sergeant Donaldson could draw breath the young lady, who had been sat quietly sobbing on an armchair, launched herself at the Chief Inspector, grabbed his lapels and said, 'I killed him. I killed him,' before breaking down into tears and falling back onto the armchair.

'I'm sorry about that sir. This is…' The sergeant was again interrupted by the young lady who seemed to have gathered her strength and once again bewailed, 'I killed him'.

Realising that the young lady probably had some important information for him the Chief Inspector decided to question her further.

'Now then miss…'

'Mrs. Mrs Davenport. I am Mrs Davenport and I killed him.'

The Chief Inspector suspected Mrs Davenport was either drunk or mentally deranged but decided to continue his interrogation of her.

'Right. Now Mrs Davenport, am I to understand that you killed this gentleman on purpose?'

'Yes. How many times do I have to tell you? I killed him.'

'Yes, but did you plan to kill him?'

'Yes. I killed him and I wanted to. I don't kill people for fun.'

'Quite. Could you tell me why you killed him?'

With a sigh of exasperation Mrs Davenport continued, 'I killed him because I am fed up with Christmas'.

'Fed up with Christmas?'

'Yes.'

'Would you care to explain?'

'Yes. Oh, please let me explain. I will tell you everything.'

'Right. Sergeant, take some notes?'

'Yes, sir.'

Licking the end of a stubby pencil the sergeant sat on a chair by the window and opened his notebook.

'Go ahead then Miss.... sorry, Mrs Davenport.'

'Well, I sat up and waited for him to come. At about quarter past twelve I heard him come in. I was waiting behind the door and when he walked in, I hit him with a frozen turkey. He fell down and I hit him again just to make sure. And there he is. And there is the turkey. They are both dead.'

Chief Inspector Cavendish looked at his sergeant and whispered, 'The turkey was frozen so what did she expect it to be?' Turning and smiling at Mrs Davenport he, assumed what he hoped was an encouraging tone, and said, 'Yes. Go on'.

'Then I went to bed. But I couldn't sleep.'

'Was it a guilty conscience that kept you awake?'

'No. It was the damn reindeers.'

'Reindeers?'

'Yes. I could hear them munching the hedge. Munch, munch, munch.'

'Reindeers? Munching the hedge?'

Thoughts of mental instability again entered the Chief Inspector's mind and he was about to ask the sergeant if he could get a doctor when the door opened and Dr Culler entered the room.

'Hello there. What have we here? Ah, Father Christmas. Well this time of the year does tend to bring them out doesn't it? It explains the reindeer anyway.'

If the Chief Inspector had not known Dr Culler for a good many years, he would have doubted the doctor's sanity as well, but now he was beginning to doubt his own instead. Fearing the answer, he nevertheless knew he had to ask the question.

'Reindeer? What reindeer?'

'Why those munching on the back garden hedge old man. Don't tell me that Cool Eye Cavendish hasn't seen the reindeer. They are attached to that bloody great sleigh parked on the back garden.'

Once more the young lady launched into speech, 'Yes. We sleep in the back bedroom and that's why I could hear them. Munching away they were. I just couldn't sleep. I had to get up.'

Going into the kitchen, Chief Inspector Cavendish and the sergeant looked through the window and saw a string of eight reindeer harnessed to a large red sleigh filled with presents. Furiously, Chief Inspector Cavendish turned to Sergeant Donaldson and demanded, 'Is this some sort of joke Donaldson?'

'No, sir. At least, I don't think so.'

'If it is then, by God, I'll have somebody for it. Christmas Eve, a dead Santa, a bloody great sleigh and eight munching reindeer, not to mention a frozen turkey. If this is somebody's idea of a joke, then they are in for a very rude awakening, my lad. Do you understand?'

'Yes, sir.'

Chief Inspector Cavendish marched out of the kitchen and back into the room where the body lay.

'Right young lady. Explain yourself. And make it good. Who is this man? Why did you want to kill him?'

'But Chief Inspector, I've already told you. It's Father Christmas.'

'Don't give me any of that rubbish young lady. Who is he and why did you kill him? Don't waste your time in telling me he is the real Father Christmas. Now out with it.'

'Chief Inspector I assure you that this is the real Father Christmas. And, like I've already told you, I wanted to kill him because I am fed up with Christmas. I hate it.'

Again, the young lady collapsed sobbing onto the armchair. By now her handkerchief was sodden and the doctor handed her a piece of cloth the size of a small pillowcase, 'Here you are Mrs Davenport. Use this.'

Thanking the doctor, she smiled and continued, 'Every year it's the same. My husband works away and doesn't get back until late on Boxing Day. I always end up entertaining my mother and my mother-in-law on Christmas Eve on my own and it's awful. They don't get on, you see, and I so wish they would. If I was a child, I could ask Father Christmas to make my wish come true, but adults can't go and see him. I've thought about writing to him…'

Stopping to catch her breath she looked quizzically at Chief Inspector Cavendish before asking, 'Do you think it would do any good?'

Refusing to take this question seriously he asked, 'When you say they don't get on, who do you mean? Your husband, your mother or his mother or all three of them?'

'No silly. Everyone gets on with Philip, that's my husband. It's just that my mother and mother-in-law don't get on. And neither of them likes me very much either. My mother-in-law thinks that Philip married beneath him and my mother would much rather be at John's, that's my brother. However, she can't stand his wife, so she won't go there, so she comes here and sulks.

'My mother-in-law walks round checking for dust, complaining about how I waste money if I buy anything and how I'm mean if I don't. Both of them complain of being bored and then whinge if I ask them to do anything, even helping with the washing up is out of the question let alone peeling any potatoes.

'They hate the presents I buy them. Last year I bought them identical bottles of perfume. I have to buy them the same present or else I'm accused of favouritism. Anyway, my mother said it brought her out in a rash and his mother said it went rancid on her. I almost told her that everything went rancid on her.

'They only come at Christmas. The rest of the year we go down for odd half days here and there, see them separately. But at Christmas I have to suffer them both on my own. It's the same every year.'

'But why murder Father Christmas? I still don't understand.'

'Simple, if we didn't have Christmas they wouldn't come. So, I decided to do away with Christmas. It was like a dream. No more thankless hours of endless cleaning, washing, ironing, shopping, cooking, washing-up. I know the two drunken old bats upstairs will hate everything again this year, just as they did last year, and the year before, and the year before, ad infinitum. So, you see, if I killed Father Christmas there would be no more Christmases. I had to kill him. So I did. I hit him

74

over the head with a frozen turkey. Has it defrosted by the way?'

Dr Culler knelt down and laid is hand on the turkey's breast, 'I don't think so. Better give it another couple of hours. Don't want to make to old folk ill.'

'No doctor. Thank you. I'd better put it back in the kitchen.'

'Just you leave that turkey where it is, young lady. It's evidence.'

'It's lunch,' Mrs Davenport cried as she leapt back off the hearthrug.

'Sorry, Mrs Davenport, but it's off the menu today. It's evidence of a crime.'

'I'm sorry Chief Inspector. I didn't think. Of course, it's evidence. You'll need to take it for tests won't you. How stupid of me. What will you think of me?'

Refraining from answering this question, the Chief Inspector asked, 'You say you went to bed, but couldn't sleep?'

'Yes.'

'What exactly were you planning on doing next?'

'Next? I suppose I thought I'd get up early and cook the turkey. I mean it's such a shame to waste such a nice looking bird. It would have to be thoroughly cooked of course.'

'You have a dead body on your hearthrug, and you were thinking of cooking the murder weapon? What were you going to do with the body? Sauté it?'

'Now who's being silly? You roast a turkey! I wasn't sure what I planned on doing with the body. Probably putting it on the sleigh and letting the reindeers take it away. I mean no one would miss him 'till next year. Mind you when I saw him lying there, I realised he was far too heavy for me to lift. I remember thinking something about getting some help from either my mother or my mother in law, or even both of them,' looking down on the still figure she continued, 'He is much bigger than I thought he'd be'.

'You honestly thought that one of the elderly ladies, who are not even prepared to help you wash up, would help you dispose of a body?'

'I don't think I was thinking very clearly. I see now that the whole idea was preposterous.'

'I'm glad you finally realise that. Now, I'm going to

take you to the station where we can take your statement and get you to sign it. I am going to...'

Much to the Chief Inspector's annoyance two matronly ladies marched into the room. One of them dressed in curlers and a green face pack whilst the other was wearing curlers and a pink face pack.

The one with the green face demanded to know, 'What's all this noise for? Do you know, Michelle, that there are reindeers in your back garden? They are making a terrible mess of your hedge.'

Sailing over to the hearthrug the one with the pink face looked at the prone figure and said, 'What's wrong with this person,' and proceeded to give Father Christmas a hearty kick in the ribs.

'It looks to me like he has had too much to drink,' complained the galleon in the green face pack.

'Really, my dear, you could have told us you were having a party,' grumbled the battleship with the pink face pack.

'This is not a party, madam. It is a murder scene...'

'Oh, how charming. A murder mystery,' shouted the green behemoth. 'I love a good murder mystery.' Turning to Mrs Cavendish she continued, 'My dear I didn't know you like them as well. What about you Miriam?'

'I love them, dear. They are so exciting. Much the best sort of parties,' the pink demon replied. 'Now don't tell me. You're the doctor and the gentleman in by the window must be the policeman.'

'I am Chief Inspector Cavendish of...'

'See, I knew you were a policeman.'

Before Chief Inspector Cavendish could reply, he was interrupted by a groan emanating from the hearthrug and the figure of Father Christmas slowly sat up and rubbed his head.

'What hit me?' he moaned.

'I did, with a frozen turkey,' Mrs Cavendish admitted. 'I'm terribly sorry. I don't know what came over me.'

'It's all right my dear. You probably thought I was a burglar. Occupational hazard I'm afraid. Happens every year. Are you having a fancy dress party? Are these two delightful creatures Jelly Babies?' Father Christmas asked seeing the two elderly ladies.

'Please meet my mother and mother-in-law. Mrs Davenport senior and Mrs Clyde.'

'Good evening ladies. Sorry I thought you were dressed up as two Jelly Babies. Must be the biff on the head.'

He tried to stagger to his feet and almost fell over a coffee table. Mrs Cavendish ran to assist him and as she put her arm round him, he winked at her and whispered, 'You'll get your wish'.

Then, aloud, he said, 'I could do with a drink'.

'What a good idea,' the pink and green jelly babies cried in unison as they led Father Christmas across the room to a well-stocked drinks cabinet.

'Do you want to charge this woman with assault?' demanded Chief Inspector Cavendish.

'No. Not at all. Quite understandable. Some strange man enters your home, quite natural to biff him on the head, eh what ladies? I think I'll have just another drink, thank you. Just a small one though please,' he hurriedly added as his glass was half filled with liquid. 'Don't want to get arrested for drunken driving, you know. Never do for Father Christmas to get arrested, especially on Christmas Eve. Got a few more presents to deliver before morning. I'll just have this, and I'll be on my way. Thank you.'

'Do you all want to stay for lunch?' Mrs Davenport asked as Chief Inspector Cavendish and Sergeant Donaldson picked the turkey up off the rug and brushed it down for any stray hairs or bits of fluff.

'NO. We do not want to stay for lunch thank you, Mrs Davenport. Come on Sergeant. Let's get out of this mad house.'

As Mrs Davenport escorted the policemen to the front door the gentle murmur of friendly voices followed her down the hall.

'I've always thought Michelle a perfect wife. Phillip is so lucky.'

'I have always been so proud of her. She is so thoughtful and kind.'

Once again, Father Christmas had worked his magic.

Late for Alf
by Lesley Atherton

So, that was it. I stretched my hand out and touched him. He was cold. I'd never thought all that much of him before. He'd been one of the many street people I'd seen begging, and the one I chose to help. I can't tell you why I chose him, but it wasn't his good manners that swung it.

I think everyone ignored him except me, but I took an unexplained shine to him. I'd usually stop and give him a sandwich and some milky tea in a plastic cup.

But this morning I was late. I took a different route and journeyed by taxi instead of the bus. I didn't see him that morning, and he didn't see me.

That day's hailstones were heavy, deafening on my office's windows, and Alf didn't cross my mind for one second until I left the building to make my way home. By 5 pm, the hail had turned to a beautiful feathery snow. I walked the five minute stretch to the bus station and looked towards Alf's usual bench. He was asleep. I walked to him as usual and laid my daily contribution by his side. It was only then that I noticed the colour of his hand and, worryingly, the lack of steamy breath coming from his mouth or nose.

Even his unwashed odour seemed somehow lessened, as if it had been frozen out.

'Alf,' I said. Commuters looked at me, unconcerned but momentarily curious. 'Alf - I've a sandwich for you. BLT today. And a brew.'

I shook his arm. Gently. He was unresponsive; cold; his eyes unseeing.

I called one of the bus drivers. Together we checked Alf. We touched his face, hopefully, but it was no use. He was gone.

I still rush past your bench, Alf - twice every weekday. And I still buy a sandwich and a milky tea in a plastic cup. Now it's Harry who takes it from me. He's one of life's casualties.

And a chatterbox - the things I could tell you about him.

Harry's alright but I've never forgotten you, Alf. I wish

I'd woken just five minutes earlier, had caught my first bus, had bought you your usual breakfast, and shared our usual morning witticism. I don't blame myself for your passing, just wish I could have helped. Or said goodbye.

Alf, I miss you.

(First published in 'Can't Sleep, Won't Sleep' 1)

Lonesome Castaways
by Jackie Hutchinson

Discarded boats cast adrift, rising tides, the sands shift.
Washed up in muddy graves, decayed, left by receding waves.

Braving the wintry gales are billowing torn sails.
Lonely masts, rigs stand alone amidst bracken, overgrown.

Under skies of gun-metal grey, lazy boats silently lay.
Amidst dark and dismal scene, is forbidding Conder's Green.

Bitterly cold and hostile, mile after solitary mile.
Little comfort in rain or sleet, this marina has admitted defeat.

Wooden slats, weather worn, desolate- they look so forlorn.
Bereft from human hands in these stark, barren lands.

Lost
by Jackie Hutchinson

Lost in a physiological maze:
which direction do I go?
longing to look outside
my comfort zone –
spread my wings,
imaginatively

Poetic thoughts
slip through my fingertips-
I must keep on writing:
pen at the ready –
no words come through;

what new poems
await in my inquisitive
            mind

I feel harmonious rhythm
obliterate before the stanzas
get to the page.

My mind's a fog
of bewildered
literary illusions

frustrated:
an emotional wall
emphasises this mental block
in my head!

There's always tomorrow…
still my literary talent
may not evolve on paper
will my resolve return?
gnawing defeat
never leaves me.

The Lost Ring
by Kath Litherland

It was freezing. Had she left the window open? Still delirious with sleep, she groaned and tried to turn over. Her face pressed against raw cold; that crunched slightly. She jacked open her eyes to a blinding whiteness. She shut them again and then opened her lids more carefully. White crystals beneath her cheek, her breath fogged. The world tipped as she raised herself on one arm. She stared at snow - Snow beneath her and around her, like a blanket on the ground; weighing down the branches of the trees behind her and crusting the ice of the frozen lake in front of her. Slowly, she got to her feet, turning on the spot.

Whiteness - Snow everywhere; tree trunks black against the coating of white. She stared at herself. At least she was dressed for winter, padded jacket and trousers, boots and mittens. Where was she? How did she get here? And how could she get home?

Beyond the place where she had lain, the snow was unmarked, undisturbed by any track or footprint. How could that be? It was as if she had floated down like a snowflake. She shook her head – there was no point worrying about that now, she had to get home.

She remembered her name – Jennifer Howey. Her parents had taken a cabin by the lake for the Holidays. It had been so exciting going out for a tree and then putting up the decorations. But then she had lost her mum's wedding ring. Her mum had said that it was OK, but she knew it wasn't.

She'd sneaked out to look for it whilst her mum was busy with her little brother. She had re-traced their steps to where she thought they had gone for the tree, but she'd got lost. The next thing she knew, she'd woken up here. Their cabin was by the shore of a frozen lake. Was it this one? If she followed the shoreline, would she find the cabin? - But which way?

She looked up at the sky, it seemed darker than before, the sun must be going down. She really did not want to be here at night. Whilst she stood there, undecided as to what to do, a light came on at the other side of the lake, straight opposite to her. Where there was a light, there would be people, and the shortest route was straight across.

There had been jet skis on the frozen lake – at least she thought it was this lake, the day before, so surely the ice would take her weight. She searched around until she found a heavy stone and threw it onto the ice as hard as she could. It bounced and slid some distance across the ice without any sign of a crack. She stepped onto the ice – it was solid. She set off towards the distant light.

The light was much further than she had first thought. She'd been walking for ages and the light seemed no nearer. But something else was closer – a fountain – frozen mid flow, the ice sculpted into an amazing tracery of fine frozen lines of spray. Something glinted amidst the shards of ice, something small and golden. It was a ring. Could it be her mother's?

She broke off the piece of ice that held the ring and held it carefully in her gloved hand.

Thinking how pleased her mum would be to have it back, she set off with renewed strength.

****

She was exhausted by the time she reached the other side. There was a small beach where she could walk ashore and then clamber up a small bank – and there was a cabin! She dragged leaden legs through the snow as she hurried towards it – but there was something wrong. As she got closer, she could see the windows were boarded over. The porch had broken railings and one of the steps had collapsed. It couldn't be their cabin, but even if it was abandoned, she could find some sort of shelter – and there had been a light!

As the evening darkened, she noticed a kind of glow off to the side of the cabin – there was a light just inside the tree-line. She made her way towards it.

There was a fence around a small patch of earth and a man stood there, holding a lantern and looking down at something. He turned as she approached and smiled gently.

'Hello Jen.'

'How do you know my name? Who are you? Do you know my mum and dad? Where are they? I got lost; they'll be so worried,'

'I'm Mikey. Mum and dad couldn't get here this year. Mum's ill and dad wanted to stay with her. It's been a long time bum-face.'

Shock raced through her. This tall man in front of her couldn't be Mikey, but only her pesky little brother at his most annoying ever called her bum-face.

'I don't understand.'

'We never found you, Jen, but you come here every year at this time. We all make the trip here every Christmas in the hope of seeing you.'

'But – but I can't be – dead! – I feel tired and cold and confused and, and...'

'Look behind you – do you see any footprints other than mine?'

She stared. The snow she had just tramped through was undisturbed.

'But I can pick things up! Ghosts can't do that. Can they?'

He shrugged. 'Maybe!'

She struggled to take it all in.

'You said mum's ill.'

'Yes, but we're hoping she'll pull through. Dad's looking after her.'

'What about you?'

He smiled. 'I'm fine. My wife's expecting our first child, a girl. I'm a Preacher.'

She looked at him. She couldn't think of a more unlikely person.

He smiled again and shrugged. 'I know; no-one expected it, least of all me, but - things change people.'

She wondered if it was because of her.

She looked down at the piece of ice in her hand. It was starting to melt. She reached out her hand to Mikey.

'Give this to mum. Tell her I love her.'

Mike took off his glove and carefully broke the ring away from the ice which entombed it. He read the inscription on the inside   Together forever.

'She'll be so happy, Jen, I ....'

When he looked up, she was gone.

84

The Magic of a Winter's Day
by Neville Southern

Storm clouds whirl and storm clouds scurry
Far behind them pale moonlight
Flickers where the snowflakes hurry
Dark the sky, and dark the night.
On and on my cold feet bear me,
Crunching on the frozen ground,
Why I know not, something scares me
In the unknown plains around.

Like a milestone, weird it glimmers
There in front, standing upright
Like a fiery spark it glitters,
Vanishes into the empty night.
Ghosts past number, formless, curling
In the play of dim moonlight
Fiends past number, all are whirling,
Like frosted winter leaves in flight.

Blizzard angry, blizzard crying,
Bodies start and shake in fear,
Further on again they're flying
In the night the eyes burn clear.
Crowds of them! Where do they hurry?
Why the song in mournful pitch?
Is it corpses that they bury?
Make they curses for a witch?

Onwards fly the demons, sailing,
Baying beastlike, howling at me.
And their howls and mournful wailing
Echo on from tree to tree.
Storm clouds whirl and storm clouds scurry
Far behind them pale moonlight
Flickers where the snowflakes hurry
Dark the sky and dark the night.

The noise drops; spirits no longer soaring
Midst whipping winds and scurrying snow
Angry with loud and stormy roaring
Regrets for what they no longer know.
Moonlight shines brightly on soft snow
In an unremittingly soundless place
And footsteps, purposeful, quiet and slow
Tread carefully under veils of white lace.

Mary's Day Out
by Sally James

Mary shuffled her feet on the wet tarmac in a slow methodical way. She had been here before; she knew instinctively only then it was the cobbles glistening in the lamplight not the neon lights of today. She was going somewhere; she was going to her home in Rochdale. She saw a house in the distance, a red bricked terraced with a small front garden and a bay window that looked out on to a busy road. She smiled and wrapped her outer clothing around her slight body, it was getting chilly and she felt the cold so much nowadays.

When I get home mother will be waiting there with my tea on the table she thought. She always does when I get home from school. Then I will play hopscotch around the lamp post with my friend Marion. She smiled again so glad to be going home, though Rochdale seemed much brighter than she remembered.

When she approached the house, she thought she saw her mother closing the curtains and waving so Mary waved back, her smile becoming broader. It seemed such a long time since she had seen her mother and felt tears edge itself from the corner of her eyes and trickle down her cheeks.

Walking up the garden path seemed to take Mary forever, she wondered how she could have hopped, skipped and jumped her way once over. She knocked on the door a timid kind of a knock and was sad that it was not opened immediately. She tried the door handle but it would not let her in, she looked under the plant pot by the window for the key but there was none there, she even felt through the letterbox for a piece of string with a key dangling on the end but there was nothing there either.

Unperturbed she turned around thinking her mother was still at the mill, a huge lumbering place that belted out cotton tea towels by the hundreds. Her mother worked in the wages office there and sometimes worked late, especially on a Friday when the wages were paid. She must be there she thought.

She crossed the busy road dodging her way between

passing cars that drove far too quickly, frightened at the loud tooting of horns. She looked for the mill gates and the wrought iron railings that seemed to lock the workers in during the day and let them out in the evening or when the shifts finished.

There wasn't even the hustle and bustle of the mill workers which she thought was unusual, no women with cotton in their hair or men eager to get home, their clogs clicking cobbles in their haste. The clang and bang of the looms didn't echo down the street either like they usually did.

Mary shivered, she needed to get warm and get out of the drizzle that was soaking her through. Perhaps mam has gone to church she thought, she did the flowers there some nights especially if there was a wedding on the following day. The church was only a short walk away; she could see the steeple dominating the skyline but no puffing of chimneys alongside it or the acrid smell of smoke.

The church steps looked dirty and litter straddled the street, there were no lights on inside and the door was bolted shut. It was always open and was a quiet place for prayer and contemplation but now it looked deserted and the stained glass windows boarded up. She didn't go in the graveyard it was too dark, so she wandered on to a busy road where the bright lights of a large building dazzled her grey eyes. The eyes that once held a twinkle of amusement but now just bewilderment.

Hunger gripped her stomach as she entered the building, the smell of baking bread enticing her to enter and she thought of her grandmother and how she made a batch of bread every other day. Fruit was also displayed and as she loved grapes helped herself to one or two as she passed by. She thought of the greengrocer who came with his horse and cart on a Saturday night with an array of fruit and vegetables and how her mother would scurry out with her shopping bag. Further along on the next counter the cooked meats looked tempting too and she thought of Tommy Wragg the butcher at the corner of the street and his delicious sausages. I'll eat this later she thought secreting a packet of ox tongue from the counter into a bag that had seen better days.

Her outer clothing was damp and most uncomfortable and seeped on to her skin but there was a whole array of coats that looked inviting and warm in the clothing department, so she discarded the one she was wearing for a smart grey woollen check coat with big pockets. She emptied her bag that contained nothing more than the ox tongue and a purse with a few coppers in and stuffed them into the pockets.

Feeling warm now, hunger once more took its toll so finding a seat in the shoe department, ate the ox tongue in between trying on some knee length boots. Finding a pair was difficult as zips were hard to fasten and laces were out of the question, however she did find a pair that she could slip on easily, but these were too big, but she did like them so kept them on.

Passers-by stared as an array of boots scattered the floor. A sales assistant frowned and moved the boots into their correct places as Mary trundled off leaving wet slippers and a battered bag behind. She caught sight of her flushed face in a mirror as she walked past and felt quite smart in her new coat and boots.

A rack of ladies' dresses caught her eye next, all different sizes and colours so Mary stripped off there and then and luckily hidden by a rack of dresses tried one on which happened to be the right size. One made of pale blue wool with a high collar was the one she must have, she decided. She left the dress on and put on her new coat and boots. She smiled at a busy shop assistant as she passed by saying 'Eeh ah'm fixed up neaw fert Whit Walks ah only need an 'at neaw.'

It was much easier trying hats on as there were so many, and she plumped for a wide brimmed hat with a red rose on the top. She felt as pleased as punch with herself. She had not seen her mother but was fitted out now for walking day, but she did feel hungry and needed the toilet. She saw a sign that said Ladies and searched for a penny in her purse but couldn't find any but what she did see on her way to the toilet was a stall selling handbags. Nobody seemed to notice the one she picked as she hovered around the stall, why this will go well with my new outfit she thought and placed her purse inside.

She followed the sign to the toilet placing a variety of things in her bag as she went along and feeling hungry took a couple of pies and sandwiches as well. The toilet was difficult to find but she also felt very tired after her shopping trip, so she sat down on a bench to eat the sandwiches. She hadn't gone out of the stores but sat just inside listening to the music which she could vaguely remember; the voice seemed like Gracie Fields or was it Vera Lynn perhaps? It brought back memories and half dozing she began to cry. People passed by some not caring but a nice lady asked her if she was alright. 'Aye,' she replied.

Mary wasn't alright at all; her new clothes were crumpled, and she had missed the sign for the toilet and was desperate to go. The store was ready for closing but Mary just sat there until a sales assistant guided her to an office where a policeman and policewoman were waiting.

'Yes, this is the woman I was telling you about,' the store detective said.

'It's all there on the screen you can see for yourself. And these,' she said pointing to a black bin bag, 'are her belongings'.

The sales assistant saw Mary's distress as she uttered 'Toilet please'. After Mary was toileted and given a cup of tea the police tried to find out her identity but to no avail. Her purse revealed nothing but the few coppers but on her wrist was a band that simply said Mary Dawber, 06. 07. 1940 Rochdale Infirmary.

Rochdale Infirmary was contacted and sure enough a Mary Dawber had been admitted for removal of a small cyst and had gone missing in the late afternoon. She gets confused at times a doctor informed them and we have notified her daughter who told us her mother lived in the town as a child so may have gone walkabouts.

It didn't take long before Mary's daughter arrived, a pale faced lady anxious and in tears.

'Mam, we have been looking everywhere for you,' she blurted out and put her arms around her mother.

'Do I know you?' Mary grumbled.

'I am Sheila, your daughter.' she replied.

Mary simply said 'Oh'.

'Just one more thing,' the policeman said, 'There is just the matter of paying for the clothes, boots and bag, or we may have to arrest her for shop lifting'.

'Oh, definitely, I'll pay,' her daughter said' so relieved that her mother had been found, and she held out her credit card.

'Eeh ahm all fitted eawrt neaw fert Whit Friday walks, dost like mi new clothes,' Mary said beaming at her daughter like a contented child.

'Well all in all with the handbag and contents, leather boots, Per Una dress, coat and hat it will come to two hundred and fifty six pounds,' the manager said with a bill of sale already in his hand.

Sheila gasped at the amount 'I well… can't …. er hmm …. can you take something back please?'

The manager shook his head, 'Sorry the clothes are damaged, and we can't do that'.

'My mother always had expensive tastes but better than being prosecuted I suppose,' she sighed as she paid up.

The manager smiled, the police departed, and the sales assistant helped Mary up from the chair.

'Come on I'll take you home now mum, take hold of my arm,' Sheila said, offering her arm.

To which Mary replied, 'Eeh 'ave 'ad a lovely day and don't ah look a real toff eawr Sheila, shops o mich betther than thi wer when ah lived 'ere, an' 'ave fixed missel up fert Whit Walks neaw,' she added.

Then taking hold of her daughter's hand like a five year old looked into her eyes and said.

'Can wi go an' see mi mam neaw afooer wi go whoam'.

Mid-Winter
by Sally James

There is no sun now,
just the jewelled sky
and a whisper of frost
on a cobweb.
I see the silhouette
of a fox on the moors
as the haloed moon scorns
bare fingered trees
rooting for secrets
in the cold dark earth.

My Christmas
by Malcolm Timms

The beds are full, the children home,
Your coffee's made and covered in foam.
It's the night before Christmas and all is still
You've worked so hard, the stockings to fill
Now they hang in the sparkling light,
Tomorrow, eyes will widen with delight.
The one constant gift I will abide,
Is having you always by my side.

Operation Snowstorm
by Lynne Taylor

They should have called it 'Operation Snowstorm' but
instead it was called, 'The Women's Institute Christmas Trip to
the Leonard Cheshire Workshops'. A bit long winded, that. I still
think 'Operation Snowstorm' would have been better.

Margo, the Institute Secretary, aka 'The Commander'
organised it, just like she organised everything else. Church and
Pensioner outings, Guides, Scouts, Cubs, Brownies, local PTA
and now the Women's Institute all fell under her command.

We were told to meet outside the Church Club on
Thursday evening where a luxury coach would pick us up at half
past seven. Everyone knew The Commander liked her troops to
be on time and as a result we were all outside the Church Club
by quarter past seven on a freezing mid-December evening. The
weather decided that, as it was a Christmas trip, we should be
provided with the appropriate conditions and snowflakes like
goose feathers whirled down, cold bit its way through boots in
order to wrap itself round icy toes and an arctic wind cut through
thick winter clothing. Thankfully, we were all duly wrapped up
in coats, hats, scarves, gloves, boots and warm woolly socks. No
coach though.

The Commander walked amongst her troops, clipboard
in hand, marking off names and calling words of encouragement
such as, 'It won't be long now,' and 'There's some headlights
down the road,' whilst muttering incantations under her breath.
By the time we had waited a little over the anticipated fifteen
minutes rebellion hung in the air. However, The Commander
was quick to quash any ideas of revolt.

Never before or since have the words, 'Nobody is
thinking of going home, are they?' held such menace.

At ten to eight Margo counted us yet again. She may
have been checking on the strength of her threat or simply
checking on deserters. If there were any they would probably be
flogged at the next meeting.

'Stand still,' she commanded as we walked round
flapping our arms like demented penguins. 'How can I count
you if you keep moving!'

Finally, thirty minutes late, the coach arrived. It was not quite the luxury coach we had anticipated. It was more of an old derelict shed on wheels. Beryl said it was probably pre-war.

'Aye, Crimean War,' I replied.

'And it's still got its original driver,' Amanda laughed as a small aged elf stood up behind the wheel.

The wizened old driver slowly approached the closed doors and shouted through them. 'They're stuck. Can't open 'em. No electrics.'

Now, let me warn you, when you're faced with thirty freezing women whose only intention is to get warm, stand well clear of closed doors. Any scrum half would have been proud of us the way we shoulder charged that door. The coach nearly went over, but with a weary wheeze the door reluctantly opened, and we all scrambled in.

'What's that?' demanded The Commander pointing to a gaping gash at the front of the coach through which the wind blew furious billows of snow.

'It's a hole,' the driver calmly replied.

'I can see that! What's it doing there? Cover it with something,' she commanded.

'Do you want to cover it with your coat, ma'am?'

'I most certainly do not.' And with that The Commander flumped down into her seat.

'Sorry ladies,' our antediluvian driver serenely announced. 'The heater's not working. Like I said, the electrics are out.'

I think the jury was out as well, busy trying to decide if he was brave or simply had a death wish.

It was obvious that The Commander was not amused by the cool attitude of our driver and it was with apparent great restraint that she refrained from hitting him and settled instead for demanding, 'You know where we're going?'

'Yes, ma'am. You just leave the driving to me and we'll get there safe and sound.'

I think the jury may very well come back with a death wish verdict!

Finally, we were on our way. Well, at least I think we were on our way. It was difficult to tell as some doubt was cast when a cyclist overtook us!

Over two hours of slow progress followed, before the coach finally ground to a halt and the driver turned off the engine announcing that we had arrived.

Looking through the windows all that could be seen were white fields and black sky, that is except for a few lights visible from a couple of houses. Apart from these signs of habitation everywhere was dark and empty.

'Where exactly are we?' The Commander enquired.

'Tatton Country Park.'

'Tatton Country Park? We are supposed to be at The Leonard Cheshire Workshops, and we were supposed to be there nearly an hour ago!'

'Not according to my schedule ma'am. My schedule says I'm to collect a group o' women at eight o'clock and take 'em to Tatton Country Park.'

'Your schedule is wrong then. You were supposed to collect a group of ladies at half past seven and take them to The Leonard Cheshire Workshops, where there was a meal waiting for them at nine o'clock, for which we are now late! Anyway, what's on here?'

'Nothing ma'am.'

'Nothing?' she shrieked.

'It's closed.'

'It's closed! Why did you bring us then?'

'If a group of women wants to go somewhere my job's to take 'em. Closed or open makes no difference to me.'

Ignoring this nonchalant reply and with an obvious effort to regain her self control The Commander asked, 'Do you know where The Leonard Cheshire Workshops are?'

'Yes, ma'am.'

'Well, take us!'

'Sorry, can't.'

'Why?' The Commander screeched.

I began to suspect that she was beginning to lose the battle, but I knew she wouldn't go down without a fight. By now she was a rather strange mixture of colours, ranging from white around the lips to black around the eyes, with various shades of red and purple in between. She didn't look well at all.

'Don't know how to get there,' the driver replied with simple honesty.

'You just said you knew where they were!'

'Oh, I knows where they are all right, but I just don't know how to get there. I knows the way from the depot but not from here. I could takes you back and start again if you want.'

Yes, the Jury has finally come back with their verdict; death wish!

'What about your sat nav?'

'Could never get to grips with one of them things. Never needed one you see.'

Through gritted teeth The Commander turned to face the passengers again and asked, 'Has anyone got a phone with sat nav on it?'

A reluctant murmur of replies ran through the old bus as a range of excuses were admitted to, 'Left mine at home' or 'Mine's flat', or 'Not got sat nav'.

'Well, has anyone got a map?' the Commander asked with exaggerated patience.

Now this particular item had slipped my mind when preparing for the crusade, but Sylvia, Margo's second-in-command, could always be relied on. Slowly her arm grew above the seats and in her hand a small piece of paper blossomed.

'There's one on the back of their hand-out,' she replied in an almost inaudible whisper.

Snatching the young bloom off its precarious stem Margo marched back to the front of the coach.

'Turn on the lights,' she ordered.

'Sorry, can't.'

'Why?'

'Interior lights gone. No electrics.'

By now The Commander was becoming quite a little chameleon.

Once again turning to face the passengers she demanded, 'Has anyone got a torch?'

Silly me, this was another item that had slipped my mind when preparing for the crusade. Mind you so had thermal long-johns and they would have been handy as well.

Again, it was Sylvia who came to the rescue. From the bottom of a capacious shoulder bag she produced a small pencil torch which was instantly snatched by The Commander who then began directing the driver.

'Turn round, go down this road for three quarters of a mile, turn left, straight down to a set of traffic lights and straight across.'

She could be very precise could The Commander when she wanted to be. However, she soon tired of giving directions and handed the paper and torch back to Sylvia.

Nearly an hour had gone by and Sylvia's slightly less than precise directions weren't exactly instilling confidence in the driver, or the other passengers either come to that. Well, you couldn't really blame us. After all instructions such as, 'I think you go down this road for about half a mile or so, you come to cross roads, or it could be a roundabout or something and I think you take a leftish straight on,' are not calculated to inspire confidence, especially as over the last mile or so the road had progressively grown narrower until now the spiky fingers of the bushes were etching the windows on both sides of the coach and a line of grass covered the centre of the road.

The final crunch came when Sylvia visibly began to wilt, and tears began to flow.

'Oh dear,' she cried. 'I seem to have been reading the map upside down.'

It was nearly eleven o'clock when we eventually arrived at the Workshops. Unfortunately, although they had remained open waiting for us, they had started to close and had reluctantly sold our meal to another troop of tourists. However, they did their best under the circumstances and managed to provide us with a welcome feast of tepid soup, a variety of slightly curly sandwiches of somewhat dubious content and a dessert of either apple pie or ice-cream which was washed down by a choice of lukewarm coffee or stewed tea.

Quite an entertaining trip really. I have booked to go to Holland in April. I doubt it will be as interesting, but I'll wait and see.

Picking Coal With Dad
by Sally James

Maggie got ready for her walk with her father like she always did on a Sunday morning when he didn't go down the pit. She liked the smell of him on those days as if her mother's soap had stuck to his newly ironed shirt and lodged in the seams. He didn't smell of sweat and dust like he did on workdays, this was his Sunday smell and when he bent down to kiss her she would notice how smooth his chin was once the bristles had been shaved away.

He smelled of tobacco too, the rough cut heavy kind that lingered in his hair and made yellow marks on his fingers. He always lit up first thing in the morning, whilst he waited for the kettle to boil for his pint pot of tea. Maggie wondered how he could drink it so strong. She liked tea too but weak and diluted with creamy milk and sweetened with brown cane sugar left over from the Christmas cake baking.

Maggie loved these Sunday mornings when she had her dad all to herself and her mother and baby sister were sleeping in the big iron bed that rattled each time she turned over in her sleep. Sometimes the rattling was so bad she wondered why this was so but nevertheless fell asleep to the musical jangling of her parent's bed.

Her father would sing in-between slurps of tea and long draws from a cigarette he had rolled himself with his coal ingrained fingers. He needed the nicotine to clear his lungs out he said one morning when Maggie grimaced as the coal fire spluttered when he spat into it.

He had been off work a week or two now, so she had him all to herself for a few hours each day before he went scavenging for work or waiting outside the pit for news to come through that the strike was over.

But they never missed their Sunday walk even in those grey days when cupboards were bare and houses cold. Despite all the odds women still went to church in their Sunday best, the feathers in their hats ruffling in the wind and their long skirts swirling in the puddles they tried to avoid. Her mother would have gone to church too if she could find someone to mind the baby, but Maggie and her father would be out walking. Maggie with her tin pram jiggling on the cobbles and her best doll wrapped up in an old sheet, her father by her side with his whippet Jack wearing the worn leather collar with a long piece of string attached.

This happiness was sheer bliss even on cold misty mornings when the low clouds hung like dirty sheets on an old washing line. 'Look at those sinners going to church,' he would laugh, and Maggie would laugh with him even though she would be decked in her finery a few hours later when she went to Sunday school.

This particular Sunday morning would be different from the rest. Her father had woken her earlier than usual the bristles on his unshaven face pricking her cheek when he kissed her.

'Come on luv, wak up,' he had cheered. Maggie didn't want to get out of bed this morning, her head felt cold and when she finally emerged felt the cold lino on her bare feet. Her clothes were downstairs folded on a chair waiting for her to dress by the warmth of the fire, but it wasn't crackling up the chimney like it usually did and the windows had iced up and the net curtains stuck to them.

'Jack Frost's bin,' her dad said with a shiver and she noticed how there was no pint pot of tea and the kettle wasn't hissing like it usually did. The only steam was that of her own breath as she hurriedly dressed.

Jack the whippet yelped in excitement when he saw the collar with the string in his master's hands and pranced up and down on the stone flags, his paws rat a tatting.

'Ere tek thi little pram, wi'll need it,' her dad said with a grin and Maggie even at her tender age knew instinctively that he was up to no good.

The three of them set out earlier than usual, there was an angry mist sloping down from the slag heaps and Maggie was surprised when instead of walking past the church towards the meadow they headed towards the pit. There was hardly anyone about, and there were icy patches in the rainbow puddles The mud had frozen and imprints of clogs looked sinister in the grey morning. Her father's whistling stopped short as they neared the slag heap. She noticed a few men scuttling in the slack, and then run off at high speed.

'Come on lass,' he whispered and together they neared the dark mass. Like the others he scuttled and foraged among the slippery slack only to emerge with a large lump of glistening coal. Three times he did this placing his treasure under the covers in Maggie's doll's pram. She grumbled at first that her doll would get dirty then saw the strained look on her father's face.

They walked back down the lane, Maggie puffing with the weight in her pram and the little dog sniffing around in case a rabbit had made its way from across the fields. Her father muttered something about acting normal as they walked past two hefty looking men one in a policeman's uniform. They smiled at the father and daughter walking out together as a pale sun emerged from behind the slag heap.

'How ert thi Alf?' the man in the policeman's uniform said.

'Ar reet Tom teckin eawr Maggie eawrt fer walk afoor er gust Sunday schoo.'

'Looks like it's warmin up a bit,' the other man said.

But Maggie thought she saw a look like suspicion in his eyes so made up as if she was cold and tired and wanted to go home.

Her father nodded and said 'See thi ert bowlin green later on, better ger er wom ers cowd neaw'.

The man in the special policeman's uniform nodded and Maggie and her father hurried on their way. They had to pass the church to their little terraced house and saw the ladies and a few men walking silently, a few nodded and smiled but Maggie's father didn't stop like he usually did. They just scurried past them and down the back lane to their house.

The house was cold and empty when they got back, and the lacy patterns were still etched on to the windowpanes, so he guessed his wife had taken the baby to her mother's a few doors down the street to keep warm.

'Come on lass lets get this fire agate afoor her comes back wom,' her father said raking the cold ashes out of the fire grate and placing the smaller pieces of coal on top of sticks of firewood and newspaper.

'The's a big cob here as ull keep us warm ar day and there's a bit er slack int backyard so wi can keep it backed up ar neet' he said his whiskered face broadening into a grin.

It wasn't long before the fire was roaring up the chimney and melting the frosted panes and the kettle singing in the flames.

'Go un fotch thi mam Maggie don't tell her why a want it bi a surprise.'

Maggie ran down the street and into her grandmother's house which was only slightly warmer than their own but at least there was tea on the table and a smell of toast warming the air.

'Come on Mam, mi dad wants thi,' Maggie urged and was so impatient that her grandmother scolded her and asked her to leave her mother alone. Maggie's mam went back home all the same wrapping a woollen shawl around her slim shoulders with the baby snuggled next to her. She expected a cold house when she got in and decided she may go back to her mother's later or maybe her aunt's who lived across the road. She got a surprise when she noticed smoke puffing out of the chimney and the windows so clear she could see inside and the reflection of the firelight dancing on the walls. She was even more surprised to find her husband sat in the rocking chair by the fire with a toasting fork in his hand and some crusty bread on the table oozing butter.

'Don't ask any questions neaw, it's nowt ter do wi thee,' her husband said as he poured tea from a brown teapot that had been kept warm by the fire.

Maggie lived to be almost eighty years of age and has long since been dead. She experienced the depression, the soup kitchens and the Second World War. She went to work on the pit brew sorting coal when she was older and met her future husband walking down the pit lane. They married had children and grandchildren. She experienced many holidays abroad with her husband in their later years, they went to countries she had only dreamed about. They bought a house with a garden and central heating, but Maggie never forgot that cold frosty day when she went picking coal with her dad.

Remembered Love
by Sally James

I have a remembered love
ticking away empty seconds
from a very cold clock.
My pendulum swings north
when the air is alive with
yesterday's magic.
I could hold him now
if my fingers were young
not wrinkled with age.
Even my heart is weak
though it still beats quietly
into another dimension
taking him with me.

The Raven
by David Jackson

High in the valley of the Harthope Burn
In a solitary rowan, the raven,
Guardian of memory and thought
Mythic messenger, summoner of souls,
Seeker of the slain, hunter of the hanged
Sits alone, in the wolf-months of the year
Waiting to see which way the world will turn

Angered by our impudent intrusion
He hauls his black-clad body aloft
And uttering his strident 'pruk, pruk' cry
Flies from rowan to rock, rock to rowan
Criss-crossing the steep sided valley,
As we wait to see which way the world will turn

Beneath his rowan roost
On grass white as frost with droppings
We stoop to gather the feathers he has shed
Black as the night, black as the pit
Together, in a place that has abandoned time
We wait to see which way the world will turn

Now, as life returns again to the frozen land
And the adders stir from their winter sleep,
To slither over the ancient graves
The raven tumbles in his Spring flight, and
We climb once again the remembered track,
Unsure where our destination lies, still
Wondering which way the world has turned.

Rinse and Repeat
by Pat Laurie

Oh, where are my specs? well, they're here on my face!
Don't let er... thingummy? er... whatsername? know.
She'll say that my memory's all over the place,
It's never, it's just a tad slow.

Now what have I come to this green, wet room for?
It'll come to me in a bit.
Can it be notes on the Hundred Years War?
I feel quite exhausted with it.

Better get dressed or I'm going to be late
For History with my Lower Sixth,
They can be a pest but I'm lucky I'm blessed
With rare knowledge of Henry the Fifth.

He was a hero at old Agincourt
When he conquered the Frenchies times three
And reopened, I've mentioned, that Hundred Years War...
Hey! Why does that woman keep staring at me?

She says she's my daughter; what nonsense is this?
I'm not even married you see,
And don't ever plan till I find the right man
To give up my teaching... till then I'm Scott free.

What is this lathery foam in my hair;
Is this why she's looking at me?
She's coming at me with that insolent stare.
Sweet Jesus, I'm starting to pee.

It must be my mother; what does she want?
I'm late and it's starting to rain.
But then... I come to... and I see I've one shoe.
Lord save me! It's starting again.

The Rivington Man
by Lynne Taylor

Rivington lay before her, its calm waters reflecting pale grey clouds floating across a pallid blue winter sky. As Sonya tried to concentrate on the view memories swamped her.

She remembered picnics with her parents and her brother, Tom. This was where they had played, this was where she had met Dan, her husband, this was where they had done most of their courting and this was where they had, in turn, brought their children, Jack and Alice, on picnics. So many happy memories but now all gone. Tears slowly escaped and ran down her cheeks.

Her parents had died over ten years ago but Dan, her beloved husband, had only died a few weeks ago.

'Why have you gone without me?' she cried, but no answer came.

Leaving her car, she stumbled across the damp rough grass and down a rugged track until she came to the path that led along the wall at the edge of the lake.

Here they had walked, laughed, played and talked. Where were they all now? Dead, she thought as she watched the grey waters lapping and slapping over the pebbles at the water's edge.

'But our children aren't,' she angrily declared. 'Why did they have to leave me as well?'

She knew the answer and already regretted her anger. They had both gone home. Jack had returned to America where he had a good job doing something in the computer industry that was quite beyond her comprehension, Alice had returned to Cambridge where she was a molecular biologist undertaking some very important work. She had tried to explain to her mother what it was all about, but Sonya hadn't really understood that either. She realised that she no longer understood or knew her children, they had grown up and moved away and moved on, leaving her and Dan behind.

'That's the trouble,' she cried. 'They've all left me behind and gone without me.'

Watching the serene water steadily lapping over the

pebbles she became engulfed in a peaceful calmness. She knew that a little way along the wall there was a protruding rock that they used to climb over to skim pebbles.

Like a magnet she was drawn to it, her mind clear and placid. Following the wall until she reached the magic spot after which she knew she would be free. Free of anger, free of sadness, free of loneliness. Freedom lay on the other side of the wall. Freedom and water.

She had just lain her hands on the wall ready to climb over it when she became aware of a young man standing at her side, but she didn't turn to look at him. She was on a mission.

'It's not freedom.'

She wasn't sure if she had heard him properly, but she ignored him anyway.

'It's not freedom, it's sadness, loneliness, fear, anger, despair. Don't do it. It's not worth it.'

Finally, she turned to look at him. He was good looking, but not particularly handsome. She wasn't sure if it was his old military grey coat that gave her the impression, but she thought he looked sad and vulnerable.

Despite not wanting to talk to him, or to anyone else for that matter, she heard herself say, 'What do you mean? What's not worth it?'

'I know what you're thinking. I know how you feel. Believe me, it's not worth it.'

'How do you know? What do you know?'

Ignoring her questions, he simply said, 'My name's Adam. I used to live at Walker Houses.'

'Never heard of it. Where is it?'

'Oh, it's quite near here. Just up there a way. It's only small. A hamlet really. My parents and grandparents, and probably their parents as well, lived there. We've always lived there.'

'I've lived round here all my life and I've never heard of it,' Sonya declared.

If she expected him to give any further explanation, she was to be disappointed.

'Your way is not that way,' he said, pointing to the lake. 'Your way is that way,' he added pointing back towards the car park at the top of the hill.

'How do you know which way is my way?' she demanded.

'I have trodden many roads and I can assure you I know. You have friends and family?'

Without knowing why, Sonya felt compelled to answer, 'Yes.'

'Why don't you give them a chance?'

'A chance for what? My husband is dead, and my children have their own lives to lead. They're not interested in me and don't really need me anyway.'

'So, they don't ring you, visit you, write to you?'

'No!'

'Do you ring them, visit them, write to them?'

His accusatory questions had been simple, but she couldn't bring herself to admit the simple truth.

'Our son lives in America so I can hardly just pop in to see him, can I? And our daughter is always busy doing some research into something or other that I don't understand. She'd hardly welcome a visit. Besides, she's in Cambridge so hardly a quick drop in for a chat and a cup of coffee, is it?'

'No,' the young man said. 'But you could still ring them.'

'Have you any idea how much that would cost, young man. I'm not made of money, you know.'

'I understand, but does that stop you writing to them? You could email, send them a text or Skype. Although I'm behind the times in a lot of ways I've managed to keep up with modern technology. Only just, I will admit, but I've kept up with it. If I can do it, you can do it. So why don't you? Too many people today seem to think that everyone else should keep in touch with them, but they don't need to keep in touch with anybody.'

They stood lost in their own thoughts, the only sound being that of the water softly slopping over the pebbles.

She knew he was right but hated to admit she had been allowing herself the agonising luxury of self pity. What would he think of her if she did admit it? She'd never met him before and would probably never meet him again but somehow it mattered to her.

Her mouth went dry and her words choked her, but she

finally knew she had to say it. 'You're right. Keeping in touch is a two way road and I've been parked on it too long. I'll give it a go.'

Shaking his hand, she turned and walked back up the path to her car.

On her way home seeing the welcoming lights of a bar and restaurant Sonya remembered it had been a long time since her cornflakes that morning and a late lunch was in order.

The pub was warm and welcoming, an open fire burned merrily in one room and she decided that a hot meal in front of that fire was just what she needed.

At the bar a smiling barman they were still doing lunches adding, 'You're looking happy, if you don't mind me saying,' as he handed her a menu.

Sonya was surprised to realise that she was happy. Happy for the first time since Dan fell ill.

'Yes, I am. I've just met a very nice young man at Rivington, and we had a lovely chat. He's quite cheered me up.'

'A nice young man, eh?' the barman grinned.

'Not like that,' Sonya giggled. 'We just chatted a while and he gave me food for thought. He's made me realise things that I've taken for granted before. I suppose none of us are too old to learn.'

'Where did you say you met this young man, if you don't mind me asking?'

'Today I don't think I'd mind anything. Just ask whatever you like. And I met him at Rivington, by the side of the lake. Why?'

'Was he wearing an old army greatcoat?'

'Now I come to think of it, yes he was. Why?'

'Did you get his name?'

'All I can tell you is that he's called Adam and lived in a hamlet called Walker Houses. He said it's round here somewhere, but I've never heard of it. Have you?'

'Aye, I have that, and I think I've heard of your Adam. Just hang on a minute, will you?' And before she could reply the barman had disappeared.

Returning a few minutes later he handed her a piece of paper and asked, 'Is this him?'

Taking the proffered piece of paper Sonya found herself

looking at an old sepia picture of the young man by the lake.

'Yes, this is him, but this picture's old.'

'That's a photo of Adam Clough. He used to live in Walker Houses with his two brothers, sister and his parents. They were a poor family, well most of them were round here. He was the eldest son and a bit of a tearaway. Always in trouble. Poaching was a common enough crime back then and he probably did a bit of fishing, taking the odd rabbit or hare, or even a deer if given a chance, but then most of them did. How else were they to feed their families, not that the landed gentry saw it that way. Anyway, Adam here got in with a bad crowd who'd come up from Liverpool. This gang intended robbing the Hall and Adam was to act as their insider. He was often there trying to scrounge a job or see what he could get, so they knew him. He was to find out when they were going away. The Lords and Ladies often did in those days, they'd go for weeks at a time. Anyway, Adam was to let them know when the Hall was empty and most of the servants would be out, so the gang could nick whatever they wanted, giving Adam a slice of the takings. He was supposed to keep lookout as well.

On the night in question the gamekeeper's wife was having her second little 'un and nobody got much sleep. The gamekeeper was walking round his cottage, not being able to settle like, and sees activity at the Hall. Knowing the family were away he goes to investigate and finds a robbery in progress. To cut a long story short the gang took fright and legged it and poor old Adam got caught. His mum and dad were right and proper upset and fair screamed at him in court saying, 'Why can't you do something to make us proud for once in your miserable life?'

Rumour has it he went to prison and when he got out, he signed up for the army and was sent out to fight in the British India Wars. He went out at sixteen and returned a Corporal when he was about twenty-six. He'd finally done it, or so he thought. He'd finally done something to make his parents proud. He was a Corporal. Only, when he went to tell them, he found his home had been flooded under the reservoir, and his parents had both died. One brother had died in the British India War in which he himself had been fighting and his other brother had drowned himself in the reservoir when his sister had died in childbirth along with the baby. Adam blamed himself, stupid boy, and went and drowned himself in the reservoir. Well, that's his sad story.'

Thinking back over what Adam had said to her she understood what he had known, although how he had known it, she had no idea. Now, she was even more determined to succeed and to do something to make him proud. Something she could and would do.

Ronin
by Peter McGeehan

I want to write about Ronin. I've never met him. I've never been to his neighbourhood. I've never been close to him. Never had his experiences or set my eyes upon what he sees. My feelings are not the same and I have made no study of him, save for what my mind and my soul will envisage in the next slice of time, which is dedicated to my new imaginary friend.

The day is crystal clear, crystal clear in the true sense of those words. The cold clear colours of white, blue, and grey, with the sharp lines defining shapes sculptured by glacial march from mountain to sea. The lightly snow peppered glacial plain is surveyed by the glistening movement of sensory eyes. Steam jets spurt from beneath lazy jowls, blowing black on the breeze over the glistening black nose. Small insulated ears twitch, listening for the faintest clues to danger or any prey. Any sound instantly investigated by the nose. The multi-layered coat hangs in knotted plaits below the belly, stained black and brown. Stout well clad legs and large circular feet are also deeply stained in yellow and grey, making Ronin appear two -toned, with his cleaner off white, upper fur. At around the weight of a small car, a cuddly friend he is not.

Ronin stands quite still, moving his head slowly, perhaps contemplating a movement, perhaps not. Why move when you don't need to? It is two days since he last ate, but he is far from desperate. He is a good hunter and free from injury and illness. His life needs are simple, to feed, breed, and to have shelter when resting. He has no natural predators, but at six years old he has learned to stay clear of man. He has detected the blood of his sister and mother near human settlements. The nearest female is some six miles away and not presently in season.

Today Ronin will dine. An Arctic storm is brewing, which would close the restaurant for up to a week.

He moves off, heading for the thinner ice. Arriving at an area he knows well he stops and puts his nose to the ice. This way he can use his most sensitive exposed area to detect sub surface movements, a lot of it. Now dribbling from the mouth in anticipation, he stands erect to eight feet, then pounds on the surface with his forelegs until the ice splits and opens up into a still black pool. The immediate surface ice cannot support Ronin's weight, so he dives without hesitation into the icy depths. He is an accomplished swimmer and quickly targets the slowest and weakest dolphin from the large selection.

The 150 pound creature is subdued and brought to the surface. Massive sharp claws enable a swift exit from the water and the prey is carried, leaving a mile long blood trail to a sheltered dining area.

Ronin, who until an hour ago stood alone in a seemingly vast unoccupied space, is now harassed by sea birds and Arctic wolves for a share of the bounty. They must await their turn, or risk being listed on the menu.

Ronin is now off white, brown, black and bloodied red. Not exactly the ideal representative of the Polar Bear, as seen in your local zoo.

Norman Winterbottom
by Ken Hahlo

Allegedly, before you die your life passes before your eyes. I, baptised Norman Winterbottom, had this experience, before being bedded in a coffin that smelt of new wood – my favourite smell as an amateur carpenter.

The vision of my life began dressed awaiting my baptism in the Church of St Nicholas, Bolton, on a cold wet day. Brought home in Dad's Austen A40, he toasted my arrival and elevation to family membership with a glass of his finest whisky. His welcoming-home speech, where he wished me a promising future, meant little to me, as aged five weeks I had more pressing priorities. As the first born, I was followed by two sisters and a brother. They were received equally warmly into the family.

My family had lived here for many years, a town noted for its cotton production and proximity to coal mines. Sadly, Granddad died in the Pretoria Pit disaster. When the mine where father worked closed, he had saved enough to purchase a newsagents' shop. With the decline of the cotton industry, Bolton became a commuter town like many others in Greater Manchester. I was the first member of our family to attend university. I recalled how at the graduation ceremony my parents, dressed in their wedding outfits, not owning anything equally smart, joined the throng of proud parents enjoying free teas and buns. On our return home, father immediately poured himself a useful helping of whisky to regain his equanimity.

Having decided upon teaching as a career, I endured further years of instruction. Having qualified, I was appointed to teach English at St Justs, a local secondary school. I taught there most of my life, culminating in promotion to the illustrious position of Deputy Head Teacher. I could not have wished for a more rewarding career. Many of my pupils went on to enjoy successful careers. John Halliwell established a plumbing firm; Margaret Black rose to the position of head typist at the hospital and Andy Greenhalgh established the finest butcher shop in town. They earned far more respect and honour than I could imagine. A few of the more adventurous achieved notoriety with the local constabulary.

My vision moved to my early years of teaching, when I met Agnes, elder sister of Dora, one of my pupils. After a respectable period of courtship, I recalled with excitement how, unbeknown to our parents, we consummated our passionate relationship during a heat wave in Blackpool. For the sake of propriety, Agnes stayed with her Aunty Cath, a lady of easy virtue, whose B & B, Home Comforts, suggested to our parents that all who sort refuge under her roof were safe from predatory males. I stayed with her divorced husband at his B & B, 'Sweet Dreams', above the door of which was written 'Nothing ventured, nothing gained!'. Returning home, we announced our engagement. As two of Agnes' siblings had left the family home, her parents insisted that we move in with them, until we could buy a house. After our wedding in Bolton and honeymoon in Southport, Agnes and I returned to work. She quickly earned promotion to the position of supervisor in India Mill 2 and I became senior master at St Justs. I recalled how, as driven by thrift, we soon amassed sufficient funds to rent and later to purchase our own house. In my vision I saw Agnes pregnant with Jeff, soon followed by Jessica.

My father exhorted us to have a large family; he favoured six children. When challenged as to why he had never produced that many, he claimed hardship. Much to the disappointment of both our families, we had only two children. I remember how Agnes and I believed this to be the modern approach to family-planning. When the youngest started school, Agnes returned to her position as supervisor in the mill. Excelling both as a supervisor and as manager of our home, we could afford annual holidays to Blackpool and later to the Costa Brava. I purchased our first car, a Ford Cortina, an appropriate car for a family of our standing. Now we enjoyed a standard of living commensurate with her promotion to Manager and mine to Deputy Head Teacher. In the light of our successful careers, we exhorted our children to embrace education as the way forward in a fast-changing world.

My vision shifted to our retirement. While Agnes became active supporting those living in hardship, I returned to my favoured hobby, carpentry. I persuaded myself that a hobby, which required physical exertion and mental expertise, would provide me with the ultimate secret to enhance my longevity. As an adept carpenter, I chose to concentrate upon coffin-making. I came to believe that there was no better way to spend one's old age than making coffins with new wood. For me the smell of new wood conjured up notions of comfort and delight. By making coffins for those in need them, I believed that I could postpone the moment when I would need one. When not making coffins, I immersed myself in local politics serving the town with distinction. As an upright and decent man, I upheld the law of the land and believed in the sanctity of all men and women. Law-abiding to the very end, I was the recipient of only a few parking fines bestowed upon me with bad grace by over eager parking wardens. I attributed this unbridled enthusiasm to those in control failing to understand the ageing process rather than to attribute it to my failing competence as a driver of a car. A blemish on my character! However, I was reassured by the knowledge that I had received two fewer fines than had our neighbour, The Hon. Alderman Ferguson Winstanley.

Having reached the ripe age of eighty-eight years and two months and still blessed with reasonable health, I passed away as a result of a tragic accident. I had taken our dog, Newsworthy for a walk. Whenever he saw cats, he chased them. On this damp day, ahead of us an arrogant black cat strode across the road disappearing under a hedge of Berberis Julianae. At a safe distance from us and with a disinterested demeanour watched our endeavours from the far side of the hedge. With an eagerness that belied his age, to remind this animal of its place in the order of pets, Newsworthy dragged me into the hedge. Still clutching the leash, our chase ended with me pinioned by thorns. The poisonous thorns set up an unpleasant reaction that led to my heart giving up an unequal struggle. Soon afterwards I died from poisoning.

After leading a near blameless life serving my community, it was in death that the ignominy of a moment's carelessness descended upon me. To my embarrassment, I was stripped, washed and dressed by strangers in my wedding suit. Agnes, my wife, said, 'We must recognise his final wish to attend the party to celebrate his life dressed in his best. It was his commitment to thrift that got him, us, through life'.

In a coffin made of new wood of my own construction,

117

lying on my back – not my favourite position – as I shall snore and suffer back ache forever, I recalled how Agnes used to tease me saying, 'If you quaffed a pint of Black Sheep, that meant fun tonight'. When I had a dram, she would say, 'I shall sleep in the spare room, as the night could be noisy'. She was a decisive woman. To be fair, I never heard myself snore. When I consulted the 'internet', I learnt that sleeping on one's back encouraged such sepulchral activity. After all, if I couldn't hear myself snoring, how could she? Generous to the end, by going first I ensure that she will suffer from no further disruptions. I have done the noble thing. Ever considerate.

I recalled when I first suffered from these afflictions. It was on my first camping trip with St Nicholas' 75th Scout Troop. The Church Newsletter referred to this initiative as a character-building experience. Ever mindful of my development, my parents encouraged me to go. Though such forms of personality development never appealed to me, Scout Leader, Edmund Greenhalgh, whom we called 'Crouchback' after the second son of Henry 111, said to me, 'Norman, I'm unsure what the future has in store for you. I can't envisage you walking a path leading to greatness, so I recommend that you sow your wild oats before you lose your ambition to succeed'. He was not a man of great vision. Although I never liked him, the idea of sowing wild oats appealed. I followed his advice. My first girlfriend, Mary, blamed me for the birth of little Edgar. Fortunately for me, Little Edgar had more in common with next boyfriend, Andy Heaton, than with me. Ethel blamed me for the birth of Hebe, a bright young thing, who had much in common with Billy Wrightington. Fortune favoured the dissolute, so I got away with such achievements. Finally, I found happiness with Agnes.

Lying in my coffin, I am surrounded by my family and friends enjoying themselves. Although unable to join in the fun, I can hear Agnes making merry. I can sense Jeff, our eldest, tucking into the feast. The consumption of food epitomised the height of his ambition. I hear my son and others observe, 'He wasn't so generous in life,' 'He didn't drink to excess' and 'I shall miss him'. I hear Agnes saying, 'In life his guiding light was 'thrift'. He washed daily, changed his underwear and never cleaned the toilet'.

I would never have believed that they loved me so much. I am proud to be dead. Importantly, I can rest knowing family and friends think well of me.

It isn't fun being at a party that you can't enjoy. I hear my cousin, Billy Longman, complimenting me. I gave him extra tuition that enabled him to pass his 'O' levels. He is the son of Uncle Weasel, Dad's name for his younger brother. He was a mean old codger, he liked to say, 'The best presents are second-hand, because they have proved that they can withstand whatever life throws at them. And they are always cheaper than new things. The least expense, the greater the joy'.

I never accepted this view.

With my farewell party going so well, I am removed to the church for the family service prior to burial. Waiting for the priest to begin, venerable Aunt Astrid, sitting in the front row reinforced with three glasses of sweet sherry, in her commanding voice asks, 'Have you found the cheque I gave Norman last week?'

After a moment of silence, Jeff and Jessica chorus, 'What cheque?'

Feeling uncomfortable, in death I would have preferred to wear clothes covered in chalk or sawdust, but Agnes had me dressed in my suit. She said that I had never looked so good as I did at our wedding. Ever mindful of my parsimony, Agnes had placed my wallet in my suit pocket, where it was closest to my heart. I recalled Aunt Astrid's words, 'You may need this when I'm gone'. It was her final present to her favourite nephew. I had intended to bank it but forgot about it when I took Newsworthy on that fateful walk. 'The cheque', she announced to all, 'was for twenty-five thousand pounds'. Aware of the existence of the cheque, the mood of the congregation changed. Clutching the order of service, all they could talk about was opening the coffin to access the wallet.

Suddenly no longer the toast of the party, I've become the culprit with the prize that everyone wants. The congregation was aware that to open the coffin before Rev. Montgomery Hilton has completed the service would bring public approbation. He, mindful of a rebellious congregation, launches into the service. Everyone squirms with impatience anxious for the service to end. Once completed, Jeff asks Father Hilton to halt the passage of the coffin to its earthly resting place.

As my vision fades, I imagine the frustration on the faces of all, as they ponder the difficulties of retrieving the cheque. Envisaging it decaying slowly gives impetus to their frustration. I can hear son saying, 'Mean bugger'; 'Tight-fisted'; 'His presents were always cheap'; 'Never spent more than a tenner on presents', 'Here he is taking Aunt Astrid's cheque'; 'Can you believe it?' Becoming angrier; their minds turn to ways of retrieving the cheque. With some members of the family venting their spleen, someone shouts, 'Why didn't he own up to having the cheque?' Another voice bellows, 'Take the lid off the coffin.' 'Whoever failed to check the contents of the wallet, owes us.' 'I am glad that he has gone.' 'What a mean sod!' 'We could have spent the money. He can't spend it where he is going,'

They turn on Agnes blaming her for not checking the contents of the wallet. To my surprise, she responds in her most mellifluous voice, 'He loved his wallet'. After a pause, she adds, 'Just as I do!' However, nobody takes any notice of what she said. Billy Longman, with bitterness in his voice, cries, 'A shroud would have been good enough for him. It has no pockets for wallets'. Jeff acts. 'I'll fetch a screwdriver from my car. Armed with it, he begins to open the coffin. As each screw slips out silently, everyone crowds around him eager to see the wallet. The crowd hisses, 'Open it.' Slowly, with a reverence that is as hollow as it is false, Jeff removes the lid. There I lie with arms crossed and a mind bereft of all recollection. Searching through my pockets he finds the wallet and holds it triumphantly aloft for all to see. Silence. Opening it, he shouts, 'Where is the cheque?' He pulls a note from the wallet on which is written, 'I'm owed this for enduring sixty years and eight months of thrift. Love Agnes.'

Turning angrily, he shouts, 'Mother!' Outside, a taxi quietly accelerates away. Proud of Agnes, I'm left exposed to all surrounded by the scent of new wood.

Shirley
by Lesley Atherton

Shirley rubbed her lower back and stretched her body forwards, then backwards and to each side. From the way she'd been forced to perch her feet while sitting on a tiny outdoors wall in a small corner of Cyril's house, she could tell that this was going to be an enormous job. It was one thing being a professional declutterer and assisting customers with Feng Shui-like decisions about furniture placement and how many ornamental figurines might be the epitome of middle-aged classiness on their hallway table, but this was something else.

Cyril. Good God, Cyril.

How did things end up like this?

Shirley had cleared a patch about the size of a welcome mat, but the house was still months away from being welcoming. She wished she'd begun in an area that was a little warmer and not as snow-covered, but there was little choice. Clearing the porch and hallway behind it was the only way to get started on this job. And today's accessible floorspace consisted of a patch barely big enough for her feet to lightly shuffle on.

It had been a huge struggle to get Cyril's agreement even for clearing such a small area.

Each item removed from its stack, each carrier bag analysed, each jam jar removed, each cobweb swept - not a decision had been made without Cyril's analysis, and without his rejection of the prospect of removal.

Back on the first day, Shirley asked Cyril about his mission. Why had he asked for her help?

His answer was clear and emphatic.

'They're gonna throw me out if I don't do it.'

Though most of Shirley's clients were the monied classes who were happy to part with hard-earned cash for the prospect of greater spirituality or a cleansed aura, an odd few were what her down-to-earth straight-talking Yorkshire woman of a mother would call 'proper nutcases'. And Shirley considered her fee, considered the feeling of achievement on the job's completion, and ploughed on with it. Rarely had the jobs stayed in her head once she returned to her immaculate three-bedroomed semi-detached home which was thankfully unsullied by additional animal or human visitors.

She shut the clutter out.

Just as Cyril shut the clutter in.

OK. She took a deep breath and leant down once more. What should have been the hallway was going to be an easy-ish part to complete. It was mainly populated by carrier bags, part-filled then knotted and thrown into the piles climbing the stairs, pushing up the walls, removing the air and adding a grubby white cloak of oppression to the already tiny room. Still, each item removed equalled some progress.

Shirley reached for one carrier bag, quite heavily filled and covered with a layer of grime, dust, cobwebs and dead insects.

Instinctively she grimaced and held the seething bag at arm's length as she carried it tentatively into the garden. This was a condition of the job. She must remove items with respect, and Cyril would 'assist her' in going through everything. Items would permanently leave the house only with Cyril's explicit approval. Shirley was reluctant to agree - after all, doing it this way would add another two or three weeks of work and expense to an already monumental project, but he insisted, and he who calls the piper...

So, Cyril, accustomed to following her and watching every one of her actions was now trailing her into the back garden. Not that you could really call it a garden as yet.

'Oh, that's from WH Smith,' Cyril commented.

'I know,' thought Shirley, 'I can read the bag'.

'I wonder what's in there,' he said.

'I can't wait to find out.'

Shirley's agreement to Cyril's conditions had come with the compromise that she refused to reach into bags to remove unknown items. She justified this by saying once she'd been jabbed by a syringe and ended up in hospital, but there were other fears her profession threw up that scared her more than the odd dirty needle. She wouldn't tell Cyril that, so simply stated she would empty all bags onto a large cream-coloured canvas sheet, now under a canopy outside the house. No reaching in to find... well, whatever.

Shirley had long given up trying to keep her nails long

and delicately manicured. She instead concentrated on keeping them short and out of trouble. The shorter they were, the more chance they would not pierce the latex gloves she insisted on wearing for each and every job of this sort. As a result, the knots closing the bags were proving hard to open, so she'd resorted to scissors. And that's what she used now. The WH Smith bag was snipped open and the contents emptied onto the rapidly staining cream canvas. It was only once the items inside were dispersed that she allowed herself a proper look from behind her disguise of tied-back hair, protective hat, air filter mask and all-covering paper suit. That's what was required on a job like this. And she didn't care how the clients felt about that. If they were offended, that was their prerogative.

The bag had contained a receipt which fluttered in front of her. It was dated four years previously, so was one of the newer bags in the house. She reached over to place the small slip of paper into a bin that Cyril had provided for items to be shredded and recycled. He took the paper from her hand. She shuddered. She hated people touching her, specially her clients. It wasn't that she didn't know where they'd been. It was because she knew only too well where they'd been.

'Can't chuck this,' Cyril said, in his customary flat, nasal monotone.

'Why on earth not, Cyril?'

The job would take the best part of a year at the rate Cyril was going. She was so tempted to simply lob a few tons of plastic bags into a secret skip under cover of darkness, because there was no bloody way that he would ever miss them.

'What happens if I...?' he began.

'Nonsense,' Shirley almost shouted. 'You don't need this - I'm putting it in the recycling. OK? You have to get used to this. Now, what's here on the sheet?'

She looked down and gently rummaged with her yellow-gloved hands, uncovering three aircraft magazines that didn't look as if they'd ever been read. Now they never would be. The pages had gummed together with condensation - or something worse.

'Unreadable,' she barked at him. 'Recycling, Cyril.'

He took the magazines and sat on them the moment she turned away.

'Recycling, Cyril,' she reiterated. 'Now.'

He did as he was told this time. But the battle wasn't over.

What else was there? A packet of rusted staples for metal recycling and a Kit Kat still in the wrapper though misshapen through melting and crushing. That was for the skip. Obviously.

'That's still good, that,' commented Cyril.

'No,' yelled Shirley in her head, but managed to hold it together long enough to snarl 'It isn't,' and to place it in the skip.

To follow were an old hat (skip), a mouldy brown paper bag (skip - she didn't even open it up to find out if the contents could be recycled) and a small plastic bag which smelled absolutely appalling even without the contents being exposed to the air. Shirley suspected with a shudder that it might have been a five-year-old piece of meat, sealed and tagged by the butcher then dropped and forgotten about. Please God, don't let that bag burst, she begged as she placed it carefully into a corner of the skip. Let someone else deal with the health hazard.

'What was that?' Cyril asked anxiously.

'Meat gone bad,' she said in return. 'Even you couldn't want to keep that.'

And so, it continued. Bag after bag; bit after bit. She would skip something, then he would recover it. Most of the recycled paper ended up back in Cyril's 'Keep' pile owing to the fact that he was going to turn it all into solid paper fuel blocks with a special tool he had (somewhere), despite not having a solid fuel burner. Shirley was beginning to despair.

She had found a carrier bag of broken and unlistenable cassettes. Cyril wanted to keep them. Shirley explained they were broken. Cyril said he'd make bird scarers from them and that he'd definitely need them one day. Maybe he'd meet a collector of old tapes and he could make a gift of them. Cyril smiled when he'd said that. Make a gift.

Another carrier bag. Smaller this time. Why on earth would anyone wish to keep a combination of the little round paper bits removed by a hole punch and broken elastic bands? What possible use could decomposing carrier bags be? Wrapping paper too broken, bent and ripped ever to re-use? Shoes too big? Shoes too small? A puppet with hideously hand-painted face, twisted strings and broken wood?

The hallway was gradually clearing. There had been one hell of a lot of rubbish - especially food wrappers and unknowable items too foul for analysis. There had also been a sizable amount that would be making its way to the recycling plant. There had been few surprises, other than the realisation that once upon a time somebody had cared about that hallway. There were still a few pictures hanging askew on the walls, and they were mainly undamaged, which was a miracle. Two gorgeous watercolours had survived, but sadly three or four handmade tapestries were un-saveable.

Even Cyril had agreed that those blankets of damp and mould could never be cleaned, which was a victory for common sense - and for Shirley. So, by the end of her first (very) long day with Cyril, she could look upon that tiny hallway with pride. It had an Axminster-style carpet which probably also went up the stairs (she hadn't cleared those yet) and plain white walls. It reminded her of almost every bed and breakfast she'd ever stayed in.

Shirley always took her own industrial vacuum cleaner on jobs, as well as her own cleaning supplies. She would return home and pile them into her large shed with its inbuilt washing machine used especially for work items. By the time she left Cyril's house that evening she was proud that the house had one area she'd recovered from doom.

Shirley had heard the argument that sometimes serious hoarders might perhaps feel sorry for the purposelessness of the rubbish around them so would gather it into a big and happy family. Other times she would hear the claim that clients would anthropomorphise their things, assigning human feelings and thoughts to decidedly nonhuman things. She wasn't sure about any of the justifications. She only knew that it was utterly foul and that her job was to re-beautify, which she did with zeal and energy. As she removed her mask, gloves and protective clothing, placing them carefully into his skip before climbing into her car, she considered how she would progress the following day.

There were three doors leading off the hallway. There was the cellar - she'd already decided to leave that till last - the kitchen, and the living room. The latter two were both equally unfit for purpose, so perhaps she should work on the kitchen next and then Cyril might be able to manage better and produce his own food. Wash his hands, even... So far, she had resisted the temptation to do more than glimpse into the kitchen. She was looking forward to getting home to her own spartan, white Bedlington kitchen with moveable island and creakingly full wine rack.

The car wouldn't start straightaway, choked, no doubt, with the bad air of Cyril's neighbourhood, but as she managed to start it second attempt (wonderful reliable Audi, she thought), she glimpsed Cyril sneaking into the back garden. She waited. He returned to the house with a handful of magazines. She could have screamed. This was going to be an impossible task. The damn man would be out of pocket by thousands of pounds and would STILL get evicted. And where would he go? Actually, she was confused about that one. How could he be running the risk of getting evicted? This wasn't a council-owned property, surely? Surely it was owned by Cyril? How could he throw himself out? Why was this even happening? And what was even happening?

The interesting thing about Cyril was that, apart from the grubby net curtains covering every window and the rarely opened front door, the neighbours would have been hard pushed to complain. The garden wasn't pristine but the condition of the few shrubs round the front was no worse than a third of the other homes nearby and they suited the place. Not only that, but the place wasn't overlooked, and the inside of the house and garage weren't visible from the roadside. Nobody would ever guess what was behind the doors.

But as Shirley pulled away from his place, Cyril popped out again. She would have to arrange for a nightly skip collection. It would cost more, but she would charge him, he could be sure of that. The last thing anybody needed was a self-sabotaging old bloke with a bad attitude. And by the time Shirley had returned home, run herself a bath and settled into the foam with a small glass of something sharp and fruity, the golden liquids both inside and out had done their jobs of calming and making her even more determined. There was no way the man would get her down. If he wanted a battle, she would give him one.

Her fleecy pyjamas were her unusual concession to comfort in this otherwise luxuriously utilitarian home. Mmm, they felt good. They smelled of lilac and passion fruit. Fabric conditioner that was top of the range, but it was so necessary. She needed to envelop herself in normality on her return from others' homes. Homes - that was a joke. How some of the people felt so loyal to the decaying bundles of crap they owned, as well as the decaying boxes they were housed in, was a total mystery to her.

Mind you, people in general were a kind of mystery to her too. She'd been on the planet for fifty-four years - but had never been married or cohabited. She'd also not had a date for probably more than twenty years, having simply given up looking and given up accepting. Then she'd stopped even considering the possibility. And after that came her realisation that she couldn't cope with what other people made. They made messes of her home and made ridiculous things happen in her head. It simply wasn't worth it.

The fragrant fluffiness of her pyjamas was comforting as she allowed her mind the risk of wandering to the subject of Cyril and his revolting, stuffed and clumsy house. Cyril who she could barely see under his layers and his smell. Cyril - ageless, faceless (she couldn't even picture him now after spending the entire day with him) and Cyril, the sneaky, weaselly man who crept outside to steal back his own possessions from a filthy skip. Cyril the Bizarre.

Sleep arrived, and with it dreams of magazines and biodegradable carrier bags.

Seven the following morning was early, but unfortunately necessary. Cyril had specifically asked her to arrive there at eight. He was an early riser (where did he even sleep?) and apparently had something to do later in the day. She wondered again about what the 'something' was. How odd that she found herself feeling curious about a client. But the thought passed and, after a simple breakfast of yoghurt and tinned fruit (no mess), Shirley packed up fresh accoutrements of her trade (mask, paper overalls and latex gloves) and made her way across town to Cyril's. It was a couple of miles away - but to Shirley it crossed another galactic dimension.

Cyril's front door was open, and Shirley could see into the hall. Things were very bad.

'Cyril,' she shouted, furiously, 'What have you done?' The hall was almost as cluttered as it was when she'd first encountered it, putting them into newer carrier bags, and replacing them in the hall. Admittedly, there wasn't quite as much there as she'd started with the previous day but even Cyril must have considered some of the items not worth keeping! Surely? She ran to the skip calling his name - but stopped dead as she got closer. The skip was practically empty - with the exception of a few crisp packets and the foul-smelling meat bag. What the hell?

That tenacious and frustrating old bugger must have climbed into the skip to recover near enough every damn thing. And for what? It made no sense. He was paying her for the pleasure of doing and redoing and redoing. Shirley ran back to the hallway and, arming herself with six bags at a time, began to refill the skip, frantically and with an increasingly angry, red face.

'What you doing?' she heard him shout.

'Undoing what you've done,' she shouted back. 'Why the hell would you do this?'

Cyril shuffled and mumbled, pulling his hat down over his eyes before looking her in the face and defiantly stating 'It's my stuff. It's my house. I'll put it where I want to'.

Shirley was dangerously close to telling him where she thought he should put it, but instead ignored him and carried on with the refilling, deciding there and then to order a drop skip with a lid. There would be far less chance of him deciding to climb in to rescue crap.

Deep breath, Shirley.

Day Two, was usually somewhat of a challenge with Shirley's more determined clients. Many would rebel. Many would complain. Some would cry, but most would simply refuse to co-operate. Cyril did none of the above. To her great and glorious surprise, Cyril knuckled under and even placed a few items into the skip himself. Shirley was a little surprised, but not too much. It usually took her clients a few more days to realise the benefits of the work they were doing - Cyril seemed to be an intelligent man - so she simply assumed he was coming to that realisation sooner than most. By the end of the day the skip was practically full and, while remembering some of the high- and low-lights of the day (Cyril throwing away a badly stuffed taxidermy experiment of a pheasant eating a fox was a definite high), Shirley finally put the key into her car's ignition at just after eight. It was a job very well done and she was completely exhausted. Bath. Wine. She would forget the meal and just climb straight into bed.

But as she lay in the Scandinavian pine forest bath with 'Clean Air' candles burning around her, she gradually recalled a few things - the secret smile on Cyril's face, the fact he wouldn't let her into the garage barn, the way he hadn't closed the door behind her when she left - but had followed her out and hovered. She jumped out of the bath and extinguished the candles before quickly shooting off an email to the skip hire company requesting skip removal and immediate destruction of contents the following day. She longed for her hunch to be wrong, but she knew it wasn't. He'd been TOO helpful and compliant. All her years of experience told her that this meant he'd already planned for his rebellion. What a fool she'd been not to realise it before.

Half an hour later Shirley was in her car, driving back to the place she'd already spent half that day clearing. The main problem was that there wasn't anything she could do other than ask, wheedle, cajole and otherwise persuade the man to do the right thing, not to waste both their time and to just accept that the future had to move in this direction. She stopped the car around the corner from Cyril's house, and killed the engine gently and without fuss. The door swished shut behind her, it being the only sound around. She was thankful for Cyril's mild deafness. She knew he wouldn't have heard it so walked, in trainer-clad feet, towards his home.

Most of the house was dark but, illuminated by a couple of streetlamps, it was obvious that Cyril was going about his business in his usual way. His white hair was sparkling with the damp air and illuminated by the miner's lamp strapped onto his forehead. Its amber orange light gave this tall, thin, darkly-dressed man the appearance of a flaming matchstick.

In his hands were bags and boxes. Some she even recognised. Some were even ones he'd chosen to remove from

129

the house himself. In the twenty minutes she stood and watched, this old and frail man removed more than forty items from the deep skip and replaced them back into his home, or into his garage barn. Despite herself, Shirley had lost all desire for a confrontation. She simply slid to the floor, back against a tree and, caring little for whatever might be on the ground underneath her, cried silently till she couldn't manage anymore.

The pity she felt for herself, for the wasted work and the wasted opportunities, was nothing compared to the pity and concern she was starting to feel for his old and sometimes unpleasant man who was so attached to his stuff that he couldn't do any different. Whatever it meant to him, this was different to her usual cosmetic decluttering jobs.

All the crap meant something to him. Perhaps it was time that she started to find something that meant something to her?

Shirley wiped her eyes and was thankful she'd chosen to come out without make up, for a change. Her hands were chilling now as were her feet. The decision was clear to her. She would resign from this job. He didn't want her, and he didn't need her. She wasn't sure of the legal implications or anything else, but simply knew she wouldn't do it any longer.

Shirley got up and breathed deeply a few times, not aware of her surroundings any longer. The night was darkening and the atmosphere dark and eerie. She couldn't see Cyril anymore and was glad. Perhaps he'd gone inside, cleared himself a patch and fallen asleep. He'd certainly worked hard that day. She was beginning to feel some affection for him and his predicament as she paced wearily back towards her welcoming car.

She woke, some hours later, she knew not where, but woke underneath a heavy weight. As her eyes adjusted, she realised that her head was pained and probably swollen and that she couldn't move her torso - or any of her limbs. Where the hell was she? Groggy from a bang on her head and from something else, she was sure, Shirley realised something so terrifying that she could barely articulate it in her mind.

She was still near Cyril. She was in Cyril's barn garage. The large wooden crates covered with bags. The appalling smell.

The empty wheelbarrows were the only relatively clean things around. She could smell straw and rotting, unpleasant things that even her preferred Scandinavian pine forest disinfectant couldn't have disguised. And at that point Shirley knew she'd been ambushed by a clever, manipulative man who'd now got every intention of adding another ambitious, clean lady to his collection of stuff.

And one mile away on a quiet road leading to the nearest village, Cyril saw an old school friend waiting at the bus stop. He always liked Trevor. They'd played football together back in the days when Cyril was fit and fast. Nobody was around. There was nobody to see.

'Fancy a lift Trevor?' asked Cyril.

Trevor hopped in and smiled at his old buddy.

'Not many of us left still driving, mate,' he said with respect, 'not many of us left'.

Cyril simply nodded his head. There weren't many of them left, but his little collection was growing and growing and growing…

'Come back to mine for a little while,' suggested Cyril. 'It's only a hop and a skip away'.

A skip. A great big bloody skip due for immediate collection.

(First published in 'Can't Sleep, Won't Sleep' 5)

If you enjoyed this story about hoarding, please check out my book, Past Present Tense, now available on Amazon.

Snow
by Malcolm Timms

Summer is long past, gone the kaleidoscope of verdant greens,
buttercup yellows and barley hues of autumn harvests.
The fruitful soil now turned by the farmer's plough to a rich
chocolate brown,
Awaits winter's icy fingers to break the clods of earth,
To take the new life-giving seeds of spring.
The washed out winter sun treads its weary path low in the
winter sky, making for far off horizons.
A rapacious northerly wind leads a train of heavy sullen grey
clouds,
Across an electric blue sky.

Human automatons scurry to and fro,
Huddling further into their turned up collars.
As they make for the sanctuary of home or work
Or any warm haven that may be their final destination.

Cars startle the liquorice coloured road,
with their harsh neon lights
fighting to beat the ever-changing red, amber, green, amber red,
of the traffic light hoard.

Drivers curse and honk metallic horns,
wishing they were on some far off tropical beach
Unburdened by mortgage, work, wife and kids.

Its dastardly deed delivered, the icy wind scurries off
to pastures new, leaving in its wake, a cohort of pregnant clouds
ready to give birth to the first snows of winter.

And there in the still night air floats the first down like wisps of
frozen purity,
each with its beauty so delicate, its invisibility to the human eye.

The advance guard slows, settling, only to be destroyed by the
remnants of latent warmth left by the winter sun's final rays of

hope.

Their work is done, the ground now chilled to accept the full
onslaught, the second wave waits in the crypt-like silence
preparing to be released.
Delinquent humans who have still to make the haven of home
firesides look up and shiver
But take heart that their loved ones are close by.

Houses decked with the bright glow of festive lights,
Where on windows small patches of mist clear to reveal the
cherubic faces of children.
Chattering and laughing, with the wild anticipation of what
tomorrow will bring,

When, with their mittened hands and warm winter coats, necks
swaddled in multicoloured scarves, their toboggans will knife
through the thick white carpet.

And men of snow, bedecked in granddad's flat cap and scarf, a
bright orange carrot for a nose, unseeing obsidian black eyes,
watch on as the children play.

The old couple standing, watching by their window mourn for
their own lost youth
And Bing sings on the radio, I'm dreaming of a white Christmas.

Snowed In
by Lesley Atherton

None of us had been snowed in before, and we weren't expecting it this time. Nobody would have come to the party on Stefan's farm, had the weather forecast been more explicit. We had obligations of our own – our homes, our families, our work. And we were stuck at Applecross Farm. Jess, an almost-out-of-control diabetic had only enough insulin supplies to last her till that evening. She lived down in the village but was small and delicate and had recently undergone an appendectomy. She was more than usually vulnerable and needed a mercy mission, so Stefan had searched out the key to the large living room windows. It was now possible to jump, or drop, just a foot or so from the window into the crispy soft snow. Who was to do it, and how?

Stefan himself volunteered. There was no real question of anyone else doing it. This was his house. It was his window. His driveway. His set of waders. He waddled into the kitchen, causing somewhat of a giggle from the rest of us: five sniggering partiers, still a little drunk from the night before. We'd turned up the previous night for Stefan's bi-monthly dinner party and stopped over, as was usual. Applecross Farm had plenty of room and was convenient for work, but when I'd woken chilled and shocked into life by the unaccustomed atmosphere in the farmhouse at around 5 am, it didn't take long to work out what was causing both. I'd sat staring out of the window till the rest of the house began to rise to oohs and aahs and comments of 'Bloody hell, have you seen outside?' The snow had taken us all by surprise by its appearance and by its tenacity and depth.

We'd all experimented at the back and front doors but the task of budging the snow was enormous. It left us with one option – that Stefan would dress in his angling gear in an attempt to get to Jess's house and pick up her medical supplies. And Jess was getting anxious.

We shouldn't really have been that worried. Certainly, Applecross was a farm in a rural area, but was situated only about a quarter of a mile from the nearest village accessible via a rocky lane which led directly to an A road. All Stefan had to do was to tramp through the snow for a few hundred yards from his living room window to the main road. Our pathway to medical supplies would be gritted and clear and the village shops would be even be open. Jess's house wasn't far off and Stefan had her key. Even if that didn't work, Stefan was somewhat of a celebrity in the village. He was friends with Hugh Whittington, a local author. Hugh was bound to be home, snug and warm. Smug and warm with a medicine cupboard full of spare insulin– enough to keep Jess going for a short while.

Still, I thought Stefan was brave. He'd always been the alpha male – the one who kept this disparate group of forty-somethings in touch, more than 25 years after we first met at Manchester University. Friends till we die, we'd predicted. None of us could believe that our first death would come about so speedily. Emma, a 19 year old undergraduate, had taken her own life by throwing herself from a landing window at the halls of residence. Nobody had known she was even unhappy.

Perhaps I was the only one amongst the remaining six of us who was thinking such sad thoughts as Stefan lowered himself carefully out of the window like a huge black rubber duck. He landed in the snow with a gentle crunch.

'How deep is it?' Jess called out.

'Up to my thighs,' he said.

'Top or bottom thighs?'

'Top.'

That was deep. But Stefan was well dressed for the weather and was a hardy, outdoorsy soul. Not a one of us was anxious that he'd not be back.

So, the five of us settled on the corner sofa. There was me – I'm Irena – sat next to my best friend Jess, and then there was the third female of our group – Issy. The men were Stefan (outside) and remaining on the sofa deliberating whether to add to the central heating by setting a fire in the wood burner, were Mark and Janesh. None of us were in relationships, either with each other or elsewhere. I was kind of surprised our strong friendships hadn't ever blossomed into something more but was relieved too. The prospect of things going wrong between us was more disturbing than I cared to admit.

Janesh was tall and still retained strong traces of his Indian accent, despite having lived in Manchester for thirty years. 'I suppose we just wait?' he said, hovering on the edge of the sofa. Would he get up? Wouldn't he? Everyone shrugged or nodded and basically ignored what seemed to be a potential call to action. We were warm and safe and knew Stefan wouldn't let us down. Janesh pushed his body further back on the sofa and flopped.

It hadn't struck me to try my phone. I pressed the screen, swiped, held it above my head, wiggled it round, but there was no signal. 'Has anyone else got a signal?' I asked. It appeared that everyone else had tried as all shook their heads.

'What about the landline?' asked Issy. What about the landline indeed? Where was the phone? We all set about looking and it took us a good five minutes. Janesh shouted us into the kitchen. The cordless phone was in the pantry on a shelf next to an unopened tin of olives and a bottle of vermouth. I pressed the phone's green button. Nothing. That meant the broadband would be out too. How were we all going to let our employers know where we were? It was already 7:30 am. I'd have been on my way to work already.

Issy shrugged and sat at the kitchen table. 'He won't be long anyway. I think we should have all gone together and got the bus in the village.'

The remainder of us looked towards our fallen comrade who had gamely struggled between rooms with us but who could definitely not be expected to tramp through snow so deep we couldn't even make out the shapes of our cars outside. Issy and Jess had been a little on edge with each other since we all arrived the previous night. It showed.

A sudden loud noise came from the cellar: a growling, mechanical yet organic sound. The cellar was where Stefan kept wine, preserves, tinned goods and the like, to see him through the winter. It seemed the logical thing to investigate. As I got up to look, Mark held my arm. 'Irena, don't…' Then he stopped and let his arm drop. 'What the…?' His gaze was directed to the outside through the kitchen window. 'What is it, Mark?' I asked. When he didn't answer we all flocked around him.

The body of Stefan was crumpled in the snow at the bottom of the hedge, only 100 yards or so away. He was unmoving and the sky's colour was no longer the shade of bright blue-grey snowy days. It was instead a deep, dark, purple-red:

the colour of congealed blood. The same colour that was haloing around the body of Stefan and, as we watched, ourselves unable to move, we saw our friend lifted by light and then we saw him no more.

(First published on the Scott Martin Productions blog –
www.scottmartinproductions/blog)

Snow-Fall
by Christine Wilkinson

Snow ascends from pristine white sky.
Gently settling on twisted branches high.
Dressed with silver thread like patterns of ice
Beneath young bulbs await spring's paradise.
Above the sparkling sun is peeping through
Melting the powdered fairy dust anew.

Star Trek Jumpers
by Lesley Atherton

S: I must confess, Captain, I know there to be something unwholesome about this unusual tradition of the wearing of Christmas jumpers.

K: Ah Mr Spock, what you fail to realise is that the wearing of Christmas jumpers has been sacred to the North American and Canadian holiday time traditions for many thousands of years. Even those of alternative spiritual persuasions, and of none, can appreciate the colourful Nordic purity of a Christmas jumper, or the simple fun of a basic snowman or a red nosed reindeer.

S: Still, Captain, I am, I must confess, uncomfortable dressed in this unusually casual and colourful manner, and my researches have yielded little in the way of reasons for this process and for the coded patterns behind the knitwear's simple yet bold designs.

K: I can help you with that, Spock. Simply remember that the woollen creations were made to express a primitive artistry amongst the womenfolk of farmers and fjord fishermen. They produced knitted motifs from what they saw around them – reindeer, fish, snow. There is nothing further to it… no code… nothing hidden. I believe the primitive peoples were enjoying the environment around them and were representing what they saw on their person.

S: But that is illogical Captain.

K: All art is devoid of logic, my dear friend. And that is why humanity enjoys it so wholeheartedly, and why Vulcan culture is devoid of it. You, being part human and part Vulcan must experience a form of constant artistic ambivalence.

S: That is not the case, Captain. I experience no human emotions and ambivalence is no exception. As there is no function to these clothing items other than the warming and covering of a physical form, any decorative element is anathema to me.

K: But surely, old friend, the Starfleet's symbol is not perceived solely as a decorative element on your usual uniform?

S: No, Captain, it identifies us one from the other.

K: I would not be surprised if the same were to be true of historical background of the Norwegian and Swedish Christmas jumpers. Don't you think: each being worn by a different tribe of people?

S: That may well be the case. But a simple symbol would be all that was required. Surely no more should be necessary than a colour, a stripe or a small symbol. This endless repetition is entirely unnecessary.

K: Then there we must agree to differ, old friend. Personally, I enjoy the rustic materials and colours. I can appreciate how these garments have been knitted to add individuality to an otherwise simple and practical garment. They are satisfying to me and many others of my species.

S: That may well be the case, Captain, but I am not the only crew member raising objections to such items being compulsory uniform for all crew for the entire month of December.

K: Nevertheless as a crew member, you must comply with these new instructions.

S: I must, Captain.

K: And you must comply with all the other newly introduced Christmas traditions.

S: Is that so, Captain?

K: Oh yes, Mr Spock. That would include the dressing of the Christmas tree and the singing of the Christmas carols, and, most importantly, the kissing under the mistletoe.

S: I am aware of such traditions, Captain, and have no wish to participate in any of these activities.

K: I understand that, Mr Spock. But orders are orders, and look what I have here!

Kirk pulls out a sprig of mistletoe and gives Spock an unwillingly-received Christmas kiss as Spock stands, unmoving still and stiffly, waiting for it to end. His next task, as soon as Captain Kirk had excused him from this unpleasantness, was to resign his Starfleet commission. Kisses were all very well, but jumpers of such extreme gaudiness were a step far too far.

(First published in the anthology, 'Another Time' by Write You Are)

Summer Has Her Beat
by Lesley Atherton

Burnt and bitten and bothered, that's summer for Jill. She hated its sticky sweat-inducing humidity, and the tiny, gauzy clothes and the 'I just don't feel right' vibe that she felt – about everything.

The bright colours and flimsy fabrics didn't feel right to her. The clinginess of underwear didn't either. Her inevitable sweaty, sticky, I-need-a-shower-15-times-a-day-unfreshness was the worst.

She would rant at her husband – 'How and why would anyone enjoy - or could anyone enjoy - this? How and why? How and why do others love it? How and why do I have to be one of the only ones to utterly abhor it?' He would remain quiet, smoking slowly, breathing smooth and unlaboured as he rested in his grandfather's wooden deckchair and turned down the volume on his hearing aid.

Jill loved autumn evenings as she would sit reading in the back garden, or would watch bats fly overhead, almost able to discern the sound of the effortless flapping of their wings over the other suburban garden sounds.

Jill loved watching. She loved sitting, snuggled on the garden bench, under coat and scarf, with a tinkling crystal glass of something red and rich. With air around her. With that cold, wet smell of plants that, exhausted, are taking their chance to rest. She loved to rediscover the empty spaces within her garden, and how the wind blew through her thinning hair.

She loved the winter and the spring but as each summer approached, Jill lost all drive and all direction. She didn't want to be anywhere or to do anything, because all that mattered was cool time and alone time.

In summer, she considers hibernation. She considers ice cream. She seriously considers aircon. But what would she miss? Not a lot. Ice lollies. Cold beer. Staying at home. Showers.

Jill knows she can have all that in winter too, and sighs. She's not a misery. She doesn't moan about much. She sees great fun and joy and calm in most things, but summer has got her beat.

She takes her cold packs carefully from the freezer and carries them to her bedroom where she prepares for the third tepid shower of the day.

Yes. Summer has got her beat.

'Tis My Delight
by Robert Eldon

He scuttles, a hunched shape like a giant spider, along the high fences that flank the small back road. Sticking to the shadows, keeping out of range of the streetlights from the main road, just beyond the bungalows, he makes its way towards the steel double gates of the allotment site. It's important he's not seen. He has enemies and it's important they don't know he was ever here. There are many who hate him, many who profess to despise him, many who would like to bring him down.

It had already been well past midnight when he'd left the warmth of his flat. And now out on the streets, the night cold is biting into his bones, slicing through the thickness of the thick plaid jacket he habitually wears.

He stops and looks around, as if sniffing the air for danger. The nearby homes are all shrouded in darkness, not a light is showing. He glances down at the illuminated dial of his watch – it says 1.00 a.m.

He hadn't been able to sleep, too many issues burning away at his brain. Too many thoughts racing through his head.

His mind turns to those who would seek to set themselves above him.

'Who do they think they are? It's always the same, they always try to make me look small. They just contradict everything I tell people. They want to make me look stupid, so folk don't listen to me. But I know things, I do. Things they don't want folk to know about. Things they and their friends want to keep quiet.'

But he knows the high and mighty ones fear him for his influence on his followers, on those who believe what he says, who trust in his knowledge, who follow his lead. They fear him too for what they half realise he is capable of doing, what he is willing to do.

Well, he thinks, with a shiver of pleasure, tonight they'll see.

Twice before, they'd suffered what would happen when he was ignored, when he drove him too far, but they hadn't taken notice, they hadn't changed their ways. They'd shown him no respect. Well, tonight he'll have to repeat the medicine.

Bonfire night had been four weeks before, but tonight he has plans to stage his own private display.

Unlocking the site gates, he slips inside. The roadway down through the plots lies before him, a dark ribbon between walls of elder and hawthorn. Walking down it, he finds what he needs, exactly where he'd known it would be. What a blow it would have been had the plot-holders moved things during the day.

Yes, it's all here, just off the roadway, a stack of small tyres and two bales of hay.

Leaving the tyres and bales where they stand, he makes his way down to the bottom of the site.

Six shapes can be made out in the moonlight.

'Their precious beehives,' he thinks. 'Well tonight I'll teach them a lesson, they won't forget.'

He drops the two canvas bags he's brought at the side of the site road. The first holds two cans of petrol, the second a beekeeper's veil and a pair of thick gloves.

He makes his way back up the hill and collects two tyres. He makes five trips in all, the last two carrying the straw bales.

Putting on his veil and gloves, he places a tyre under each hive. Their inhabitants have retired for the night, but he's taking no chances. He pushes corks into the hive entrances, the bees are trapped.

Now he places straw into each tyre and soaks the straw with petrol.

For a time, he stands there, master of all he surveys, savouring the feeling of power, relishing the impact of what he is about to do. He thinks how 'they' will feel.

He moves forward again and lights the petrol-soaked straw under the first hive. The flames lick upwards, the wooden base and sides of the hive catch fire. The trapped bees stand no chance, they're incinerated.

After a long pause, he moves on and repeats the process with a second hive, and then a third, a fourth and a fifth. He feels the power in his hands. He feels, what was the word the therapist he'd been sent to had used? – 'justified'. Like everyone else she'd misunderstood him, not realised who he truly was. He'd prefer to use the word 'fulfilled'.

But as he moves on from the fifth hive, he stops. He can hear a sound on the night air. A siren, it's getting louder, it's getting nearer. Someone has 'phoned the Fire Brigade, perhaps someone from one of the houses that ring the site or maybe a late night motorist on the nearby main road. He has to make a decision. What is he to do?

His sense of self-preservation tells him to make himself scarce.

'Time to move,' he mutters to himself. 'Shame about that last hive, though.'

But he knows he must be calm. There's no sign of panic in his movements. Putting his veil and gloves back in the canvas bags, all the while listening to the sound of that ever nearing siren, he calmly picks up his petrol cans and makes his way through the site back to his own plot near the side wall. He slips into the sanctuary of his shed and sits on an old stool in the darkness, looking out of the window. He watches as the fire tender arrives and a couple of firefighters disembark. He watches as the firefighters use bolt-cutters to cut the lock on the main gates. He watches as they pull open the gates and the fire tender moves slowly through the gap and travels carefully down the site road towards the blazing beehives.

It doesn't take the firefighters long to extinguish the blaze, and maybe twenty minutes later they leave the site.

He emerges from his shed and looks around to make sure that there's no-one else on the site and that he's safe from discovery. Then he walks slowly over to the scene of the fire. Five hives have been completely destroyed and in their haste the fire crew has sprayed the sixth with a thick coating of foam.

He laughs, 'Looks like they've done my job for me.'

One more scan to make sure he's still unobserved, then, nervous of meeting someone coming in through the main gates, he slips away through a little-used side entrance. He walks home, through silent, empty streets. Half an hour later, safely back in his flat, he climbs into bed and falls into a deep, untroubled sleep.

At 8:00 am he's back at the site.

He watches as the beekeepers wander amidst the devastation. He sees the woman burst into tears and be comforted in the arms of her neighbours. He sees her husband kick the charred embers in anger and frustration. He feels a sense of achievement, his plan has worked to perfection.

He watches as the reporter from the local paper takes snaps of the debris. He sees her question the beekeepers and some of the plot-holders who are standing around in the morning cold. There'll be a piece in tomorrow's paper with the photos. He'll cut it out, keep it in his scrapbook, gloat over it in the evenings in the solitariness of his room.

Half an hour passes, and he watches as two local PCSOs appear. They want to speak to the Site Secretary. The Secretary isn't there. The PCSOs cast around aimlessly, approach a couple of bystanders, and are directed to the beekeepers, still standing by the embers of their hives. The PCSOs ask a few desultory questions, utter a few platitudes and then wander off towards the main road. There's nothing they can do, vandalism like this isn't a priority for their superiors. There'll be no investigation, this case will be closed by lunchtime. They know they'll be the ones facing the angry questions at the next Area Forum.

He eavesdrops, half-hidden, by the wall of the Council Hut, as a group of women discuss the attack. The women grumble at how useless the police are these days; How they're not interested. How they'll just say it is kids from the estate, but they can't prove it. How they'll tell the plot-holders they need to install CCTV. Advise the Committee to petition the Council to improve security, for all the good that ever does.

And then the women start to argue as to how odd it is that the same family's been hit three times in a row. First it was their shed, then their greenhouse, now their beehives. A couple of the older women voice their view that the arsonist could be someone on this site, someone with a grudge.

He looks at the speakers. Such talk is dangerous. He begins to feel as if their eyes are turning his way. Time to slip away.

But as he gets into his car, he turns and looks back at the group of women who are now opening up the Council hut so they can brew tea for themselves and the beekeepers and their helpers.

He looks closely at the ringleaders, memorises their

features, perhaps they too need to be taught a lesson.

But for now, the café at the local supermarket will be open and he's earned a hearty celebration breakfast.

Useless!
by Jackie Hutchinson

Matt grey days of winter
echo my demeanour;
bitingly cold November chill
only reinforces
my despondency.
Empty pit of hopelessness
never leaves me.

One of many thousands on
the 'scrap heap;'
tears spring to my withdrawn face.

Stuck...
at a psychological
crossroads:
'unemployed'-
is this social label
round my neck for ever?

Pounding the concrete streets;
can't go home to a silent house-
those four walls...

Sea of melancholy faces
drift in the Job Centre;
vacancies -
eyes desperately scan posts:
they're *must* be something there for me!
Letter of anticipation
drops through the door:
'Your application has been
Unsuccessful'.

Not another rejection!
why won't somebody believe in
me!

'Twas two weeks before Christmas
by David Jackson

I look out of the window, out across the rain soaked car park. It's dark outside, the lights from the College building are reflecting in the puddles. The weather's been awful for days. Sleeting down and freezing cold, still, that's Ilchester for you.

I look at the clock on the staff room wall. It's 5 pm. Just an hour to go and I'm on. Four hours until I'll be heading home.

Sometimes I wonder why I stick at this job. Still just a couple of weeks before the Christmas holidays then I get four weeks break. Staff room's pretty empty. Just us unlucky sods who drew the short straw. Thursday evening, 6.00 pm to 9.00 pm – the ultimate graveyard shift.

I've got Logistics III – a bunch of bolshie warehouse staff who definitely don't want to spend their evening here, in this draughty converted mill listening to me drone on about control of inventory and managing despatches and oh, the list goes on for ever.

Some weeks you just pray that the pyromaniac in Meat II will set fire to his copy of the 'Sun' under the fire alarms and that we'll all get a break as we're evacuated out into the car park, until the all-clear sounds. In this weather, I'd probably get hyperthermia or pneumonia. Still, that'd be a week off at least.

It costs the college £3000 every time there's a false alarm. Another ten and they'll have to sack another part-time lecturer just to balance the budget. Maybe it'll be me, then some other poor sod can try keeping Logistics III in order for three hours each Thursday.

Couldn't face the canteen, and anyway there'd have been little left at this time of day – I'll grab some chips and a pie on the way home. Better not drop in the pub, been doing that a few too many nights recently.

Better check the slide set – check the handouts. A wise man once said that a lecture is a mechanism for passing information from the notes of the lecturer into the notes of the student without passing through the brain of either. You just crank up 'PowerPoint' and print out the handouts – with the slides and the notes – you give them that and they're happy –

well not happy but they don't grumble as much.

It's not even like they're my notes, they're Bridget's, she should be teaching this lot, but she's off with 'stress-related illnesses'. Lucky sod. Probably stuck a pencil up each nostril and her knickers on her head, to fool the medics. So, I've got her notes and her classes.

They made me teach a class in Sexual Harassment last term – bloody nightmare – half the women in the group decided to recount their experiences in graphic detail. Sharon said that the storeman in the bakery where she works always leaps on her and throws her down on the flour sacks when she goes to get a new order.

'Whatever do you do?' asked Carole from the Housing Association.

'Depends how I feel and if I've got the time,' said Sharon.

Carole said that was a disgusting attitude and told me I should exercise some discipline in my classes. Sharon said she was up for a bit of discipline, as she looked good in a basque. As they used to say, I made my excuses and left, well left the subject anyway.

What is it this week, again? Ah, stock management, well that can't be too bad, can it?

You never know though, last week in NVQ3 we did Customer Care. Big Ray who works in a caravan repair company told us about a couple who brought a caravan back because the bed had collapsed. Big Ray looked at the rather overweight middle-aged couple and said 'Were you shagging? What d'you expect, the two of you banging up and down on it, it wouldn't take the weight.' Ray's on a disciplinary charge at work now.

So 'Stock Management' – vital to the smooth and profitable running of your company.

Set of headings on slide one – first is Data Capture – no risk of innuendo with that is there?

I wonder if Sandra will be wearing that blouse again – the one she was almost wearing last week? You don't know where to look at times, a man could easily lose his train of thought, and much more if he wasn't careful. God, I hope I don't have to do the residential weekend with this lot.

Last year in North Wales poor Del had to barricade himself in his bedroom on the last night and even then Brenda from Meat II, filled with lust and Jaeger bombs, tried to scale the side of the building to get at him.

'Perpetual Inventory' – not a clue – better read the lecturer's notes on those slides – ah, the age efficiency process – mine's an inverse relationship, my age goes up and my efficiency goes down, and the retirement process – God I'd love a retirement process, a nice golden handshake, a handsome pension and I'd be off to the sun, no more Logistics III. Fat chance, I'm in the wrong job for that, should have been a banker.

'Avid Cross-Referencing' – don't ask, just don't ask.

Can't follow the next one – something about 'Intercompany' – inter-company what? – oh, I see, well we'll face that when we get to it.'

Here's FIFO – always liked FIFO and LIFO – it's like JIT – I like these abbreviations – as long as modern slang hasn't converted them into something sexual or racist and the whole class starts sniggering and some po-faced sod from Human Resources reports you to the office – SNAFU was a good one – fits this place. And then 'Shelf-Life' – think I'm past my shelf-life.

'Warehouse Systems' Supplier Price Lists' – the only supplier most of this lot are interested in is the one who provides their recreational drugs on a Friday night. There's a thought, maybe I could get him (or her, we embrace gender equality) to come along on a Thursday, then we could all take things a little easier.

There was that old Tom Lehrer song, 'The old dope peddler'. Wonder if anyone listens to Tom Lehrer anymore. He's lecturing in Theatre and Song-writing at some university in California these days, far cry from Maths at Harvard. Did you know he wrote 'Magic E' for Sesame Street?'

And finally – those wonderful words that lift the hearts of lecturers and the spirits of students – and finally – 'Integrated Systems'.

Oh, God, it's nearly six, better go down to Room 3.61. Where's the pyromaniac when you want him?

Vladimir Davidovitch Ossilinsky Must Die
by Robert Eldon

In the silence of the pitch-black chapel, a single candle gutters above the altar.

The priest takes an ancient wooden casket from a hidden cupboard. He opens the casket and takes out an ancient wooden handled revolver. Taking five silver bullets from the casket he loads them into the chambers. As he does so, he recites an old incantation, brought by his forebears from the Old Country. He recites it fervently, for his life, no, yet more, his soul, may depend on its efficacy.

Outside, in the ancient winter-cold kirkyard a patch of blackness, darker and more intense n its surrounding, slowly moves towards an elaborate gravestone. The shadow is carrying something, something heavy.

As it reaches the gravestone, the shadow lays down the body of a young girl upon the slab. Her long silken nightdress catches a stray moonbeam. Her long dark hair frames her deathly pale face and spreads out across the white marble of the tombstone.

The shadow looks up to the moon. For a brief moment its face is illuminated, it is the face of an immense wolf. Its eyes blaze with a yellow light and its jaws drip blood.

In the chapel, the priest turns. He has heard a noise outside. Holding the revolver against the crucifix that hangs across his chest, he moves to the side door of the chapel and slowly descends the flight of steps into the kirkyard. He walks down the short path towards the tombstone. He stiffens as he sees the body of the girl. He cries out, 'No, in God's name, no.'

The shadow moves out into the moonlight. It begins to straighten up into the figure of a man, Vladimir Davidovitch Ossilinsky.

The priest holds the revolver out, pointing the barrel at the figure before him. He looks into a face that is exactly like his own.

'Can you really do it?' asks Vladimir, 'Can you kill me, brother?'

The priest is transfixed, 'Can he do it? Can he destroy the evil that his brother has become?

The priest stands as if waiting for a sign, a signal from God or Fate?

Then the church clock strikes, the quarter hour.

The priest stands straight and pulls the trigger. The silver bullet penetrates the heart of Vladimir Davidovitch.

Vladimir falls to the ground.

Vladimir Davidovitch Ossilinsky dies.

The priest bends down to the body of the girl. She is his niece, his brother's daughter. And now he weeps, for both are dead. He stands and begins to walk back to the chapel.

He does not see the girl's eyes spring open. He does not see they are the colour of blood. He does not see her move to the side of her fallen father, nor see her whisper something in the dead man's ear. He does not see how she gazes along the path. Towards the chapel, towards his retreating back.

Vladimir Davidovitch Ossilinsky lies where he fell. The hard boards beneath him are beginning to hurt his hip, but he must remain motionless as the light fades away.

Then, suddenly, all is light and the sound of hands clapping and people cheering. Vladimir gets to his feet, joins hands with the Priest and the girl and together they bow to the audience. Our play is over.

Vladimir Davidovitch Ossilinsky is going to die: every night this week at 10.15 pm and also at 4.00 pm on Saturday for the matinee performance.

Waiting
by Sally James

I am waiting for Spring
but all I hear is rain
throbbing on the windowpane
and wind whining
around the tree you planted
when we were young
and the sky was blue.

Streetlights dance in the dark
as if stars had dropped from the sky
strung themselves like
a row of diamonds around
the neck of the moors.

Tomorrow, will arrive
bleeding over the quarry;
a red slap of a sky, the air
will sting with bitter dew
but I will still be here
waiting.

Washing Day, 1947
by Sally James

it was like that then
mam scrubbing mangling
boiling whites in the copper boiler
mist on the windows inside
smog on the windows outside
lobscouse cooking on the gas ring
a pint pot of strong tea
to keep her strength up
me crying with measles
her raw hands soothing me
giving me medicine
in between pegging out
wet clothes in the damp air.

What a Picture?
by Christine Wilkinson

Reclining on twisted old oak tree.
Is a ruby coloured robin, singing cheerfully.
Surrounded by snow-glazed trees in winter dress,
Sparkling with frost shining to impress,
The groups of people, walking in the countryside,
Muffled in scarves, and thick coats. Suitable for outside.
Looking up as they hear robin's melodious song,
Stopping to listen before hurrying along.
Some snapping a picture, to show to their friends,
Before setting off to cosy homes at journey's end.

Eating a few crumbs left by the dwindling crowd,
Robin returns, breast stuck out very proud,
Preening himself, whilst sat on old tree stump,
On Christmas card position, beside old water pump.

When There Is Only Love Left
by Sally James

There is nothing left now but love.
When the sky changes from blue to black
he will be with you.
His head will rest upon the curves of your breast.
His lips touch the nape of your neck.
The tricks of nature will have misled you
but there is goodness in the seasons.
Each blade of grass is measured.
Your hair will fall like braids of gold upon
his shoulders and though your seeds will
no longer scatter the earth,
your arms will never be empty.

Winter Beach Barbecue
by Sally James

She placed moss and fingers
of driftwood on damp sand,
tried to light a fire
but the salt breeze wouldn't let her.
She could hear the swish behind her,
the heavy breathing of the sea
and the crackle of a flame
as candle wax dripped
on to scorched wood.
Firelight twitched and flickered
warmed her cold face, flashed
like lightening in her eyes.
She cooked sausages, drank
Irish beer and sweet French wine
laughed in the moonshine.
Smoke got in her eyes, made
tears fall, his eyes were wet too,
but she never noticed,
carried on stirring the pan
in her old country ways
till the tide turned. Next day
she walked along the beach
saw the white ash inside
the ring of stones.
'Look,' she said,
'Everything has gone'.

Winter
by Sheila Farrow

Vivaldi's version
Does it for me,
With staccato icicles
Of minor keys.
His soaring strings
Pierce the vortex
Of swirling snow.
Vivaldi's Winter does it for me.

Winter Wanderland
by Sheila Farrow

Puddles crunch
Dime Bar brittle
Underfoot.
Hands flexibly impaired
Freeze in fingerless gloves,
And friendly chatter
Sends signals on the air
That all is well.

Winter Wonderland
by Christine Wilkinson

Mountain peaks, scattered with glistening snow.
Stalagmites, stalactites up and down in a row.
Forming lacy patterns in places rare,
Where droplets of snow have pitched up there.
On old stone bridge beside frozen lake,
Resembling ripples on a special cake.

How beautiful the undulating countryside,
Hedges dressed in frosty splendour beside,
Paths filled with footprints, big and small,
Tread by young and old, a walk for all.
Children proud in well-bobs in splendid coloured hue,
Aiming endless snowballs, scoring a hit or two,
At well-known people, muffled in scarves and walking gear,
Enjoying the winter sunshine, happy to be here,
In such a wonderland of ice and snow.

As the weakened sun begins to set, it's time to go,
Back to cosy homes, where fires do glow.
Reflecting on how their magical day went,
In winter's filigree fairyland, in fun and laughter spent.

Wooden Cabin
by Lesley Atherton

His cabin was wood-walled, wood-roofed and wood-floored. His heart was wooden too, if you chose to believe the constant accusations of ex-partner jo (jo with a lower case j). She had not been a Presley fan, but Jake had, and her painful German accent as she sang 'Wooden Heart' to mock his lack of extroverted displays of affection, hurt him badly. She didn't even get the point of the song. It wasn't about that at all. How dare she get it so wrong?

They'd split up. Of course. No relationship could survive such Elvis-abuse.

So, Jake had travelled, inspired by the solitude of Thomas Merton and Henry David Thoreau. Emulating both, Jake pared down his life and his possessions. Life was about thinking and being. It wasn't about having people (jo) and having things. That wasn't real life at all.

At Walden Pond, Thoreau had removed a beautiful found stone from his tiny, self-built cabin. The joy of owning the stone was outweighed by the responsibilities of its ownership. jo (with a lower case j) had considered their relationship as one responsibility too many. Jake had been her stone (stone and wood, how very elemental!).

And so, to leave his sadness behind (for you see, his heart may have been pine or elm-constructed, but was definitely not unfeeling), Jake travelled long distances and eventually settled into this tiny wooden cabin almost perfectly suited to the complete enclosure, protection and healing of his broken wooden heart.

Jake read Into the Wild - the story of an idealistic young man's spiritual adventure of anti-materialist joy - and soaked up the sentiments of Thoreau as if each written word was food to his starving soul. Nature, self-reliance, making do, simple living and total introspection - those were what he desired, and they'd be far superior to the purely physical bliss he'd experienced with lower-case-jo. To use Thoreau's words, 'I wanted to live deep and suck out all the marrow of life... to drive life into a corner, and reduce it to its lowest terms'. And that was Jake. Or so he'd thought.

You see, the problem was that the cabin, like Thoreau's, was only a couple of miles from its nearest town, and that was not nearly far enough. Because this nearest town was where jo (with a lower case j) lived. Jake's travels had almost brought him home. Accident or design?

But this wasn't his only problem. You see, his dream had been of autumn: the harvest-time, abundance-time, warm-evenings-by-the-fire-time, but his reality proved to be one of winter-time: hunger-time, lonely-time, and chilled-mornings-chopping-wood- time.

Life was uneasy. Mind was unsettled. Some days he felt thoughts expanding to fill all the empty space around him. Oh, those days! Revelatory and purposeful, those thinkings could cure cancer, eradicate famine, and bring new planets into existence. But on other days, those head-in-a-vice-days, the pain and pressure of simply placing one foot in front of another or slopping canned food into a saucepan was too much to bear.

And tears threatened to rot his wooden heart. The wooden heart of the wooden puppet whose only wish was to be a real boy. With a real girlfriend.

He'd been eight months at the cabin when it happened. Lower-case-jo, the hiker and almost-adventurer came walking along the public footpath which passed his cabin. Her surprise as she saw a bearded and dishevelled Jake collecting water from the lake (how unhygienic!) was short-lived.

Composing herself, jo (with a lower case j), said 'Hi,' and, white-faced and unaccustomed to visitors, Jake stared back, wooden heart completely intact. How surprising!

How? Why? Because that was the day he stopped believing. He stopped believing that someone else had the power to hurt him. He stopped believing that he was worthless and that his heart was cold and hard. He stopped believing in running and hiding and started believing in confronting and co-mingling. Imperceptibly, day by day, he'd stopped believing only in her, and had started, once again, to believe in himself - and the world out there. Such adventures to be had!

jo (with a lower case j) had carried on walking. Unconcerned, Jake entered his wooden cabin with wooden floor and wooden roof, and steadily, but with increasing enthusiasm, began to pack his canvas rucksack. He would soon leave the shack forever.

Pinocchio was a real boy.

At last.

(First published in Can't Sleep, Won't Sleep 1)

Printed in Poland
by Amazon Fulfillment
Poland Sp. z o.o., Wrocław

49976544R00099